UL BORÎ • BARDAȘ • BRAȘOV • ROMANIA • juillet 1972

Published by Black Sandal 2013
41 Oriel Road
London E9 5SG
www.blacksandal.co.uk

ISBN 978 0 9564360 23

Into the Hill

For Jim

The foetus is the property of the entire society. Anyone who avoids having children is a deserter who abandons the laws of national continuity.

Nicolae Ceausescu 1966

Prologue

When Ha Ha created the world and put the people in it he said to Jap and Rie 'Now I will give you one more gift, if you use it wisely it will bring you great happiness, it will make your judgements fair, it will let you see into the heart of things, it will fuel your curiosity, it will make you wary, it will help you to question, to dissect, it will lead you to reason. This gift is Doubt.'

Jap and Rie lived happily and wondered what this special gift was all about as they could find no use for it. Sometimes they played a game where Jap would say 'I doubt my children are mine,' and Rie would call them and say to Jap

'Look at his little nose it is a copy of yours, or look at her golden curls, they came from your head, and put your hand on my heart and feel it beat for you; and besides whose else could they be?'

One day they met Mollen in the forest who told them many fine things and Rie used her doubt to be wary of his truthfulness. Then Mollen said 'You know why Ha Ha gave you doubt don't you?' They shook their heads. 'It is because he wanted to keep the best of all attributes for himself. Do you know what it is?' Jap and Rie did not. 'It is Certainty.'

'What is this Certainty?' they asked.

And Mollen answered 'It is the antidote to fear, to indecision, to confusion, disquiet, faltering, perplexity. Join me, I have built a chapel in the woods, there I can bathe you in the waters of Certainty and you will never need to doubt again.'

She shivered behind her rock; at the top of Mam Tor it was cold even out of the wind. Below her she watched birds in flight, gathering and parting, the wind blowing them off course. She would like to fly, her arms outstretched thrust upwards, her left arm, short and stubby, causing her to wobble, to almost crash into the rocks, but then gaining balance, lifting, soaring upwards to join the others. She shivered some more and considered lighting another cigarette, but they tasted funny in the open air. They were worrying about her; they'd have to explain her absence even if they didn't care. Today she knew for certain and the knowledge felt good. A rabbit crossed her path and ran frightened down the slope and disappeared into a burrow. She despised hers. *It was quite difficult in those days and we had some major disappointments*; she had never belonged, and now she knew she was not theirs anyway there was no comfort in the burrow *The first little baby girl we were given died,* fuck them all, now she could please herself. *We looked further afield and you came to us from faraway Romania.* So what if she made her mother whimper? She'd stolen her in the first place, it was so unfair, she wouldn't let them take Susan from her though. *You see although you are our beautiful little girl we didn't actually make you like Susan.*

From where she sat she could see a green Toyota. They couldn't see her, later there would be mountain rescue, and helicopters, and dogs would sniff her still warm, lifeless body, from her crack in the rock. Para-medics would radio down to the police and her parents in the car park, the TV would interview them in their distress; but the dog wouldn't leave her, he kept sniffing and making little soft barks; someone yelled 'I think she's still alive!' The helicopter was called back, she could hear the noise of the blades as a stretcher was lowered, then wrapped in tin foil, like a Christmas turkey she was lifted swinging above the peak, flying, flying . . .

A climber was using her special route up the Tor, red woolly hat. After a while, *Jen-nif-fer*, watching the hat bobbling along, *Jen-nif-fer* it shouted gaily. Fuck off growled the rock, squeezing further into the niche, shivering.

'Whachudoin?'

'Nothin.'

'Aintchecold?'

'Yeh.'

In the rock, breast to breast, one anorak, gloves shared, hat swapped. 'Have you run away?'

'Yes.'

'Why?'

''Cause I'm adopted. I'm Romanian.'

'Wow! Where's that?' They squeezed each other tighter still, and vaguely heard a car horn floating up from the car park. 'Can I run away with you?'

'No. You must go home. I don't belong. I'm a foreigner.'

'But you are my sister.' Through a small crack between the rocks they could see their mother start up the proper track, the one the walkers used. She had her hiking stick and stopped at the first bench to rest. The girls slid out from their hiding place and stood at the summit. She saw them and waved her stick. Joining hands, Jennifer held her good arm out like a wing, and Susan the same.

'I am the power,' yelled Jennifer, 'and I am the glory,' Susan followed, 'one two three,' and they ran furiously, on track and rock and scree, oblivious, screaming 'I am the power, and I am the glory,' past their mother and into the car park. Collapsing out of breath and laughing hysterically – 'for everaneveranever . . .'

.

1

More to herself than to him, 'White rabbits.'

'What's that?'

'White rabbits, that's what you say on March the first, it's good luck. And hurry up in the shower, I've got to be in the office at eight-thirty.' Jennifer had been running her own video production company specialising in fashion for the last two years, she'd been able to set it up with a small inheritance and despite the recession it was prospering; her partner Bill ran a second-hand bookshop on the Caledonian Road, which wasn't; they lived in Stoke New-ington in a house they'd bought together.

Bill fetched milk from the doorstep, they still delivered here, he loved that, in his mind it made it a proper home. Wet wind whistled up the side of the house, a dustbin had blown over, he got soaked righting it. In the kitchen he made himself a bowl of cereal, no point doing anything for Jennifer. Waiting for the kettle to boil he looked through the window at the damp lawn and a few daffodils braving the elements. They hadn't started on the garden yet, that was to be this year's project. He could hear Jen-nifer moving about upstairs on the bare boards, clearly rushing, as usual. 'I'm going to be late, be a darling and call me a cab,' she yelled down to him. Bill didn't like the frittering of money on taxis but did as he was asked.

She clattered down the stairs on high heels, 'Damn damn bol-licking damn, where did I put my work bag? Don't worry I've found it. Fuck there's the taxi, you'll have to build something out-side for this bike it takes up all the hall. Don't be late tonight, Susan's coming round, see ya.' The door slammed and she was gone.

He finished his cereal and emptied the dishwasher, there was no rush, it was going to be a wet cycle ride to the shop, and being honest he knew it didn't really matter when he opened up. The buying and selling was mostly conducted on the internet. So

Susan was coming round, Jennifer's dopey drunk sister, he thought she was still in rehab at Jen's expense, another money niggle.

At her office in Shoreditch, her team were already at work when Jennifer arrived, and were waiting for her say so on graphics and a recent edit. She dealt with the immediate business then shut her door, and opened her machine; hers was the only enclosed space. She scrolled down the business stuff to find what she was looking for: *Emile Nastase, looking forward to her visit, get flight to Cluj, please take taxi from airport.* Her heart was speeding. Sally, standing in front of her desk, was going through a list of tasks, Jennifer hadn't heard a thing and had to ask her to start again. 'Oh and Sally,' she called after her as she left, 'I won't be coming back with the team, can you get me a flight from Budapest to Cluj?'

'Sure. Where's that?'

'Romania.' She was slightly disappointed he would not be at the airport to meet her, maybe he didn't have a car? So much she didn't know, so much to discover.

She bounced around the office all day, surprising her colleagues who were used to something more focused, business-like; she found herself singing in the supermarket as she gathered ingredients for the night's meal for Bill and Susan. She hovered by the champagnes, but decided it was a bit mean on Susan, and got a bottle of Chablis instead.

She was singing in the kitchen when Bill returned and parked his bicycle in the hall. 'You sound happy', he said and kissed her.

'You're all sweaty, get away. Susan will be here in a minute.'

'Hide the whisky.'

She hesitated about whether to put a wine glass out for her sister. She could hear Bill in the shower, there was no privacy in this house. The doorbell rang, the hollandaise was about to thicken, she let it ring, Susan shouted through the letter box, Bill thundered downstairs with a towel wrapped around his waist. 'Can't you hear the bloody door?'

'Sorry.' And Susan stood in the hall with a bunch of service station chrysanthemums. She looked slightly pathetic, it had the effect of making people want to gather her up. The sisters hugged each other.

'Why the flowers?'

'To say thanks; and I missed your house-warming.'

'Gosh it's been six weeks. How was the rehab?'

'Oh, you know, sitting round in circles, moaning!'

'Mind the bike.'

Jennifer kept her secret safe all through the meal but when they'd finished eating, judging the timing like an experienced actor, taking her cue from Bill's compliments on her cooking, she decided to tell – at that instant Susan picked up her cigarettes and Bill said she'd have to go in the garden. The moment missed she felt deflated.

'I've got a work trip to Budapest next week, checking locations.'

'Wish I had your job,' Bill said and picked up a catalogue.

When Susan came back in, shivering, Jennifer said, 'I've got something to tell you both.' Bill looked up from the catalogue. Both their eyes on her expectant, a sudden bizarre thought, that they imagined she was going to say she was pregnant, made her blurt the news more hurriedly than she had practised.

'I've had an email from someone who says he is my brother.'

'Oh God, not another one; now we're all on the world wide web there are relatives turning up all over the bloody place; chap I know discovered his father was a bigamist, really caused a family rift till they found out it was all a hoax,' Bill said.

'I think this could be real.'

'You could have a brother. . . there was this bloke in rehab and he looked just like you . . . we talked about . . .' Susan trailed off, Bill looked furious.

'Go on then, what's the story?'

'The first email was a fortnight ago, he said he'd found my web site, apparently his mother, my mother I suppose...'

'Hey hang on . . .'

'Well, whoever she was, had this child, who he said is me, so the child, who could be me was put in an orphanage, because his, our, mother couldn't cope, and at that time certain children could be found homes in the West. Not exactly legally.'

'In the West! Where does he live?'

'Romania.'

'Christ Jen, it's a scam!'

'I don't think so, he knew about my arm.'

'So what, it's fucking obvious, he could have found that out easily enough, there are pictures of you out there, the one-armed camera woman.'

Jennifer continued, ignoring Bill. 'So I'm going to meet him.'

'What?'

'I can easily tack it on the end of next week. He lives in Transylvania.'

'Amazing,' said Susan. 'Son of Dracula. How exciting!'

'No, it's dangerous and stupid, that's what it is,' Bill said and he started clearing the table, banging the dishes around as he filled the dishwasher.

'Just like you to pour cold water on it, that's why I didn't tell you straight away. You've got family, mum and dad and brothers and sisters and grandparents and great uncles that go back to the battle of fucking Cressy you tell me. If there's a chance I've got a brother I'm not going to ignore it.'

'Good on you Sis!'

'Well at least get a fucking DNA.' He slammed the door as he left the kitchen and in the post argument lull, Susan poured herself the last of the wine.

'To your brother – Cheers!'

2

It was eight o'clock on a March morning, when the taxi driver said he couldn't take her any further. He pointed to a track, and said the name of the village 'Rosu.'

'How far?' she asked, he shrugged. She struggled out of the car with her luggage and set off with her heavy case in her good hand, and a bag of presents on her shoulder. She was held up by deep mud, it clung to her shoes like the Cheshire clay in the fields where she had grown up with Susan. The taxi couldn't have got along. Around her the fields were bare; black earth ploughed for the winter, steam was rising as the sun warmed them; beyond the fields, mountains, like a giant's bay surrounding a black, quiet sea.

A horse and cart pulled off from a field ahead and waited. The driver gesticulated for her to climb up, he got down, took her case and slung it in after her. There was a pile of dung at the end of the cart, the smell evoked a memory of a childhood holiday, riding donkeys on the beach. She sat among the dung and the tools they had been using in the fields, old fashioned scythes and hoes and looked at her designer trainers, covered in mud, and wondered what she was embarking upon.

When they reached the village, children ran behind shouting and holding out their hands. The man reined in the horse and she understood him to be asking where she was to go, or maybe that she should get down. 'Do you know Emile?' She said first, then 'Is this Rosu?' He said nothing but helped her down and set off carrying her luggage. She followed along a side road that was even muddier than the main track; she had to hold onto the fences that marked the gardens of the single storey houses to prevent herself slipping. Each house was joined to the next by a solid wooden gate which had a smaller gate inserted, where these had been left open she slid forward to find a handhold and noticed that the houses were bigger than they appeared on the street, stretching back like a row of cottages. Some well maintained, but many collapsing in from the farthest outhouse with only the main part near the road looking habitable.

Her farmer had stopped at a gate ahead and was shouting. A man in his forties, dark, medium height, opened the gate within the gate, her carter pointed at her struggling in the mud. The two of them talked. Was this him? Her blood? Money was exchanged and the dark man took her luggage and called to her.

'Come in, Janufa.'

She crossed the road, striding the deep ruts and looking at her feet. Self-conscious, she stood just inside the gate and the thought that she could have grown up here crossed her mind; she held onto the thought, like a small insect cupped gently in her hand, to show a child, before it escaped. Further down the yard was an apple tree with some hens perched on low branches, beneath them, two geese stared at her honking aggressively. Emile guided her across the yard and into the house. 'I am Emile,' he said, 'So happy you are here.' Jennifer was introduced. 'Our eldest boy, Alexandru, his brother Raul, and my wife, Merta.' Jennifer bent down to take off her muddy shoes, Raul darted forward and placed a pair of embroidered slippers by her feet. The single room was tidy, a bed against one wall, a table with an embroidered cloth and four wooden chairs, a bench and cooking arrangements in a corner. The bench, the chairs and a chest, were all painted with patterns or flowers. In her world it was quaint. She couldn't help making a mental note – perfect place for a summer fashion shoot. His wife was standing with the two young boys who were about six and ten years old.

'You are Emile?'

'Very pleased and grateful for your journey and safe arrival.' He shook her hand, his wife crossed herself and prayed. Emile continued, 'Taxi should have brought you, they are rubbish company, I will return you safely to the city.' She was surprised his English was so good.

'I have to be at the airport by five p.m.' she said. He eased her towards the table and the woman, Merta, placed a glass of tea in front of her and sat down. She looked older than Emile, forty-seven perhaps, quite lined with rough heavy skin. She wore a headscarf and a padded waistcoat over a blouse and skirt. Jennifer smiled across at her, it was furtively acknowledged.

The light from the door was suddenly filled with another presence, a man, taller than Emile, not as dark and rounder, softer, perhaps a little younger, stepped inside. She noticed her case had been put behind the door. The men talked together fast and with no introductions. Jennifer was ignored, the two children stared at her and one of them reached out and touched her short arm. She dived into her shoulder bag and brought out the hastily bought airport gifts of chocolates and shortbread and gave them one each. The children opened the packages, their father turning his attention to them, made the children hand round the biscuits before he introduced her. 'This is Boian, also your brother.' She gasped and stood up and this man kissed her on both cheeks.

'I didn't know I had two brothers.'

'Boian will take you to see our father.'

'Whose father?'

Emile smiled, 'Your father and our father.' Jennifer stared at these two foreign men, brothers, now a father?

'I have to get to the airport by five p.m.' she heard her voice like someone else's, noted how inappropriate but couldn't get beyond it. 'Is our mother alive?'

'She died five years ago. Stomach cancer. Boian will drive you, I have to work. When you return I will be here and will accompany you to the airport. By five p.m. yes? You can leave your bags here they will be safe.'

She sat in the front of the rusting car, it splashed through puddles the size of ponds, across ruts that juddered the suspension. She found she was trembling, her jaw so tense she didn't trust herself to speak. There was nothing to prove that any of this was anything but a charade. But for what reason? Well she wasn't a fool and she was not going to give them money. She looked across at Boian, at this stranger, this foreigner.

Boian shouted in broken English through the din of the car 'Are you cold?'

'Yes,' she lied to cover her trembling, and in the effort of speaking bit her tongue. She tried again 'How old are you?'

'Thirty eight years,' he laughed, 'two years older than you, but hard life.' He knew her age, of course, yet it surprised her.

'How far to our father?' Jesus how ridiculous that sounded.

'Our father is ill, I take you to hospital.'

'Oh. What is the matter with him?'

'Many things, his . . .' he waved his hand across his body. 'Many things, much pain. He is very magical man. He says he cannot die until what is lost is found.'

The car hit an almighty bump and Jennifer was jolted forward. 'Sorry terrible road, not like England eh?'

'Is this why you searched for me? I was lost? How was I lost?'

Perhaps he didn't understand. He drove on in silence for a while. She looked at his face, a large slightly hooked nose, eyes set far apart and narrow, black in his beard area. A face that belied his warmth. This is my brother she kept saying to herself to see how it felt, but she felt nothing. They were in a town, on a slightly better road. He stopped the car.

'Very very bad story; our father sold you to western tourists. Our mother took us away, never spoke one word to him again. Many years we live in same village but no speak to him. Then she died, and the man, our father, became ill. I visit him, bad, bitter man, he called our mother names, he said there was no money for our sister, he said he made a sacrifice for you to go to better life. We get out now.'

She squeezed out of the car, there was no pavement and the car was parked against a concrete wall. Boian led the way through a low ceilinged vestibule. There was a dreadful smell. She tried to cope by identifying the stink, something Bill had taught her when they were travelling together; cabbage, rot, shit, disinfectant?

She followed the man she had just met who said he was her brother. In the ward there were two rows of iron beds, some with shapes and crumpled sheets, some empty. Smell identification was not working, she tried sounds; wheezing breath, coughing, footsteps, her own heart beating. Boian stopped by a bed. She told herself to see it as a photographer, to observe and record, non-involvement.

A sleeper; visible above the covers, a skull, no hair, and a claw grasping the sheet; a woman in a green overall; a screen drawn round the bed. Boian spoke to the creature in the bed and it moved. The claw reached for something on a side table and offered it to her. He was living yet looked dead, his grey skin was taut except for the eyelids which were swollen and flickered, his mouth gaped. She leaned and took the card he offered and as the stink of his breath hit her throat, she vomited onto the broken linoleum. Spinning she sat down on the bed. Two faces loomed at her closely; there were open pores and hair, women, two green uniforms, talking at her loudly. A glass of water was offered and pills. She took a drink. 'Sorry, so sorry,' she mumbled, as Boian, her brother held her, held her.

'You need fresh air.' His arm supported her down the ward. She was on the street, still apologising.

She found the crumpled card later as she waited at the airport, she smoothed it out. It was a photograph of a family. The man looking uncomfortable in a suit standing next to his wife with two small boys, one on each side and in the woman's arms, a baby.

3

At the check-in the girl behind the desk asked in heavily accented English whether anyone could have tampered with her luggage. In the second that passed before the automatic response a grumbling unacknowledged worry suddenly barred its teeth.

'It's possible,' Jennifer said quietly.

'They could?' the airport woman was taken aback by her answer.

Within seconds a security guard was holding her arm, her suitcase was removed from the belt, her hand luggage taken, and other passengers herded to the other end of the hall. She felt guilty like a child being taken out of class for some giant misdemeanour, and fearful for the outcome. She was moved swiftly without option out of the public area, along a white corridor, past closed doors and into a small windowless room where a uniformed woman sat near the door. Jennifer was told to sit on the only other chair. Her questions were met by blank silence. Twenty minutes went by, she would miss her flight. Bill would be waiting.

The door opened and a second woman came in and asked Jennifer to remove her clothes. 'I need to see someone from the British embassy; I have a right to representation. Please can I have my telephone returned?'

'Remove your clothes please.' The woman by the door stood up, she had on a green uniform like the woman in the hospital. Jennifer took off her jacket, the woman went through the pockets and dropped it on the floor. 'Shoes.' Jennifer stripped to her underwear; the green uniform searched everything and piled them on the chair. 'Now those.'

'No, you can see there is nothing there.'

'It is necessary.' The uniform stepped towards her; Jennifer took them off. 'Now bend over please.'

'No, get away from me!' She fought but in seconds the green uniform had her held over the chair and the intimate search was completed. Sobbing, and totally humiliated Jennifer slid to the floor.

'You may dress now.' The woman made a telephone call, told her that nothing had been found and that if she would follow quickly her bags would be returned and she would be assisted through check in and onto the 'plane. Seven minutes later she was in her seat with seconds to take off.

She sat rigid, engulfed in embarrassment. During the flight she re-wrote the last twenty-four hours many times to build in her mind a kinder, nobler picture of herself, to excuse her awful lack of trust. She had only told the truth after all. Then blame settled on Bill and the infection of his damned contagious cynicism.

At Heathrow, back on home soil, she sobbed, her body shook all along the connection corridor as she followed the signs to immigration. In the baggage hall a woman asked if she was all right. She went to the Ladies' to wash her face before meeting Bill.

He was pleased to see her, and was clearly sheepish about his former distrust. She told him the outline of her visit but even if she had wanted to tell more she couldn't, the guilt of her loss of faith was a lump of clay worse than the Rosu mud.

Two weeks later Emile wrote with the news of the old man's death. He had fulfilled his own prophesy and lived until she was found, and reunited with her brothers. Jennifer made arrangements to attend the funeral.

It was while she was in Romania this second time that Susan turned up at Bill's shop on the Caledonian Road. She had only been once before and then she'd been drunk, but she found it all right, sandwiched between a flower shop and the North London Cats' Protection League. She walked past twice before going in; she knew Bill didn't like her. Inside it was dim, the space filled with shelves floor to ceiling with hardly room for a person to walk between them, but as usual there were no customers.

Bill was cataloguing in the office. He heard the door and came through surprised to see her; he didn't think she'd ever been in the shop since the launch, when she'd drunk and shouted, making a total ass of herself so that Jennifer had had to get her sent home in a taxi. 'Come in the back, I'll make tea. What brings you here?' He said with a manner not as encouraging as his words.

'Thought I might buy a book. No, only joking!'

Bill cleared a space and set out mugs. This was his world, it didn't make a penny, but the rent was cheap, and anyway Jennifer's company was able to support the venture against tax. 'Jennifer's in Romania you know,' he said. 'Gone to her father's funeral.' He looked across at Susan; did she go along with this? He couldn't tell.

Tea was poured and Bill talked about the weather; the cost of plumbers; the cats that inhabited their garden, disguising his apprehension at her visit. Inevitably they talked about the Romanian family. Susan said, 'When I was in rehab we used to have to stand and say things about ourselves and I talked about Jen and her being adopted and how we used to make up stories about where she might have come from. Later this chap, a care worker, was really interested and asked me more about her, you don't think that might be connected do you?'

'I shouldn't think so,' Bill said 'It would be a bit far-fetched don't you think?'

'And there's another thing I keep thinking about, when I was about fourteen and sort of shagging around and having huge rows with mum, she said that I'd end up a fifteen year old prostitute in Liverpool docks, like Jennifer's mother.'

'Ah,' Bill drew in breath. 'Have you ever told her this?'

'No. I didn't think it was true, and if it was, it spoiled the stories we made up.'

Jennifer spent five days in Transylvania this time and returned in very different mood. Bill collected her from Heathrow, he said that Susan was coming round and bringing an Indian take-away. They were quiet in the car. Silently, she compared the green flat landscape on the edges of the M4 to the mountains of Transylvania, where she had travelled with Boian.

They'd hired a car one day and he'd taken her up to The Red Lake, he'd told her its history, how it had formed twenty years ago when a dam broke. It was an eerie place, the tops of the pines still emerged from the water, some skeletal and, surprisingly, some still holding their needles, as though they had succeeded in changing their element. After walking around the lake they found a track leading up into the mountains. Boian knew all the mountain flowers, and showed her clumps of gentians and anemones. He told her stories about himself and Emile as boys, they hadn't always got on, and she wondered what a life it would have been for her, growing up as the younger sister. They drove home via the Bicat Gorge where the rocks overhung the road like tunnels. You must come to England and see where I grew up, she had said to him and he had shrugged at the impossibility of such a venture.

That evening she was invited to the house of a neighbour where villagers were making the food for the funeral. In a small kitchen seven head-scarved women added minced meat to rice before taking handfuls and wrapping them in vine leaves. Jennifer was given a place at the table. The women talked and joked and smiled at her.

The following day she walked with her brothers behind the coffin, carrying a candle. The same cart that had brought her to the village the first time was now carrying her father in his coffin. The village people followed behind. In the entrance to the church the procession met the priest who wore a long black robe with a hood; villagers came forward to take the casket from the cart and to Jennifer's horror the lid was removed. After the service, the mourners filed past the body and kissed the cross the priest was holding. Jennifer bowed her head but could not look on the corpse of her father, confused that she had already attended the funerals of those she had called Mum and Dad. When everyone had paid their respects the lid of the coffin was returned and the procession continued to the graveyard. There was a sudden wind and the day which had been sunny turned cold. The women, Boian translated, said in their country it was a good omen. Later, in the basement of the church the food prepared the previous evening was laid out with local wine; accordion and fiddle players in traditional costume played and Jennifer met relations, everybody it seemed was a first cousin, or second cousins, or cousins and aunts first and second time removed; she couldn't understand a word most of the time but it didn't seem to matter. And then there was Emile and his factory.

Jennifer told them all this as they spooned their meal out of foil dishes laid on the bare table. 'Anyway what's really exciting is that the next day I went with Emile to his garment factory. It's pretty basic, but has huge potential. It could be extended, and materials and labour are cheap there. It would need completely refurbishing of course and all modern machines put in.'

'Hang on Jen, have you got involved in this?' Bill asked.

'You bet, family business! I'll supply the templates, probably send a couple of designers to work out there. We need the real authenticity of it all; embroidery; good material; padded jackets, stonewashed to get the subtlety. They would need to work from the local colour and landscape. Emile has access to good fabric. I would then import the clothes and find markets for them in the West. I think it could be really big. All the trends are about ethnicity.'

There was silence, no one had eaten very much, Jennifer because she had hardly drawn breath in her excitement. 'Well what do you think?'

Bill said 'I've been to Macclesfield.'

'Oh?'

'You know, where you and Susan grew up.'

'I know where Macclesfield is.'

'Well I spent a day there, in the Registry office, it wasn't too difficult actually, once I got the hang of it, the registrar was very helpful; anyway I've got a copy of a birth certificate for you. Your mother was called Marie Sullivan and she was 15 when you were born. The father was unknown. You were registered as Jennifer Sullivan which was why it was difficult to find you but we cross checked with adoption records and there isn't any doubt. You were adopted at 5 weeks by Alan and Deborah Bates.'

'And when I was in rehab, I talked about you, said about the adoption and that we thought you came from Romania, so maybe someone got an idea . . .'

'Shut up Susan, you always have to be in the drama don't you.'

'Look,' said Bill, 'my time ran out up there but I know the score now and I'm sure with a bit more research I can set up the computer at work and find the links, we could discover your mother, if she's still alive, I mean she'd only be fifty. There's always records.' Silence fell again. Susan broke it.

'What are you going to do Sis?'

'I thought I told you, I'm going back to Romania in five weeks. Meanwhile I'll write the business plan, find investment for the factory development, set up the design team and research the market. I was going to invite you both to come but it doesn't sound as if you'd be interested.'

'They are not your family, Jennifer.'

'If you say so.' There was another silence. 'But neither, come to that, are either of you.'

4

Susan was awake, she had been awake for some time although her eyes were squeezed shut; she was fighting to get back into her dream; there had been a crossroads, her mother was walking ahead, and she couldn't catch up; it wasn't a pleasant dream but anywhere her unconscious drove her was better than the daily fight against addiction that was her life.

She needed to pee, she tried to ignore the sharp tickle but it would be answered. Out of bed, eyes closed, hands in front, door, edge of basin, she reached the lavatory by feel. The bathroom was cold, the drains smelled, wet towels from the last user were draped over the bath. Back in bed and counting; when she'd had her appendix out she'd only managed to get to eight before blissful oblivion; she'd been eleven and her mother had blamed her for spoiling the family holiday. Typical of little Miss Drama, her mother had said, yet loved relating the story to her friends at the club; the race to the hospital, the appendix bursting on the operating table, her anguish at nearly losing her daughter.

She had not heard from Jennifer since the Indian meal, it had been eight days…seventy-eight, seventy-nine… She got out of bed, in the shared kitchen she counted the water into the kettle, ten was enough. She checked her 'phone, it was nine forty, and no messages. There was an open, half bottle of wine on the work top. The kettle, began to sing and splutter, ten had been too long, steam engulfed the bottle of Merlot, there was no cork, she could smell it, fuck, fuck, fuck, she couldn't resist; as she reached, the steam from the kettle scalded her hand. Fuck! She knocked the bottled which rolled onto the floor but didn't break. The wine formed a puddle round her bare feet as though she were standing in a pool of blood. She put the bottle in the bin, now repelled by the smell; she used a dirty tea cloth to mop up the spill, rinsing it under the tap, one two three four, squeeze, back to the floor, and again, turn the tap, count, rinse, squeeze, she left the cloth in the sink.

Back in her room she dressed from a pile of clothes on the floor, she would go to the shop, she would see Bill. Her decision gave her confidence in the bathroom. Ten for the water to run warm, plug in basin, seven both hot and cold together. She dipped her flannel in the water then touched the soft wet soap swimming in the dish and wiped off yesterday's make-up. The black round her eyes smeared and the soap stung. Cold tap, one, two, three, four, five, squeeze and wipe. Now she had decided, nothing must get in the way. Make-up, in her bag, she'd do it on the tube, or bus, or tube. Oh God which? The ninety-one went past the shop, but it took her twelve minutes to walk to the stop. Caledonian Road tube was possibly nearer, she hadn't checked, why hadn't she checked when she went last week? She drew it in her mind and walked it and then drew the route to the ninety-one and walked that, seemed the same, it couldn't be, she was getting more and more anxious, she sat on the bed and counted. Eighty-eight, eighty-nine, ninety, ninety-one; ninety-one, she would go by bus. In her bag, make-up, oyster, keys, tissues, 'phone; five, re-check, go.

She needed a job. She'd told them in re-hab that she'd got a job. She'd said she was a P.A. in an advertising company.

Bill was at the shop. It was Thursday, a week since the terrible row which had begun after Susan had left and continued over the weekend. By Sunday they were both strung out and exhausted, that was when Jennifer had said they should part. At first he hadn't believed her; he'd woken with 'flu on Monday morning and stayed in bed. Jennifer had left early and returned late; she had asked him how he was and if he wanted anything before she had settled down with a whisky to watch the News, after which she had gone to bed, in the spare room. On Wednesday she had said she would continue to support the shop but would he find somewhere to live as soon as possible. He was stupefied . . .all their hopes. . .

The parcels were piled up on his desk in the back office; Mrs Fernandez had been in to clean and had left them neatly stacked. His scissors were handy in the desk drawer and he unpacked each book and ticked it off in his ledger of orders, he had a nostalgia for the pen. His nose streamed, tissues felt like sandpaper on his nostrils; he found paracetamol in the little kitchen and returned to his work. *A Midsummer Night's Dream,* and *Twelfth Night* with original drawings by Heath Robinson and in excellent condition. *As You Like It,* with drawings by Hugh Thompson, good too; a first edition Rupert Brooke; *Taylor on Golf* by John Henry Taylor, another first edition, and signed, that should fetch a bit if he could find the right buyer; others, of lesser interest, he'd forgotten ordering, but they were there in the ledger in his neat handwriting. The books made two haphazard piles on his desk. He sat, staring at nothing, overwhelmed by a misery so physical it froze him from the inside. He worshiped Jennifer, he adored her, he didn't see how he could exist without her, words repeated in his brain; *Perdition catch my soul But I do love thee!*

They had met backpacking, Jen, taking a gap year post university, himself just aimlessly continent hopping, hoping to find himself and he found her, in an ashram in Northern India. *And when I love thee not, chaos is come again.* It was her fucking sister, bloody fucking interfering woman he said out loud and felt better for it. If she hadn't poked her nose in here two weeks ago, he wouldn't have gone pissing up to Macclesfuckingfield, and they would all be planning a trip to Romania right now.

He had to get on with internet sales, the shop needed to make a living. He turned on his computer, plenty of email inquiries, some orders, work focus took over and the hours passed. A couple came in the shop and he sold a 1939 third edition of *World Famous Paintings.* Feeling a bit better, he put a 'Back in half an hour' sign on the door and went to the café two shops up for a sausage sandwich.

'How are you darlink, not seen you much this week?' Cosima was Polish and had run the cafe for years.

'Had the 'flu, Cosima, how are you keeping?'

'Too much work, not enough money, you get me a nice sugar daddy yes? Usual?'

On his way back he picked up a free local paper from the newsagents, he must find a place to live. He sat in the back scanning the ads. The shop door sounded, he went through.

'Hello Bill, how are you?' His heart sank.

'Been better, how about yourself?'

'Feeling a bit shitty actually.' Susan suddenly knew that coming here was a mistake. How could she have imagined that seeing him would help? 'Haven't heard from Jen, she doesn't answer my calls.' Bill said nothing 'Well I was just passing, thought I'd call in.' She stayed rooted to the spot.

'Shit it's raining,' Bill brushed passed her in haste to bring in the trays of cut price paperbacks displayed outside, she followed him. 'Let me help,' she grabbed a second tray and bumped into him coming back out, all the books slipped to the floor. 'Damn you,' he said as he stepped over the pile to fetch the last tray. She started to put the books back, 'Leave them!' He yelled. She stood up, mascara running down her cheeks and left the shop. Before she was level with the cafe he reached her. 'Sorry, let's have a cup of tea.'

He bought her a bacon sandwich as well, and told her the situation with Jennifer. They talked about her, and each being with someone else who loved her and understood the pain of separation, was comforting for them both, and in that comfort they believed that the light that was Jennifer could not be extinguished from their lives. Then feeling easy with one another they went back to the shop and together tidied up the books that had fallen on the floor, and put the trays outside again because the sun was shining.

Bill said, 'Do you think it was the person in your rehab who got in touch with Jen?' Susan described the process of sharing that was part of the therapy and how she had talked about her mum always preferring her elder sister even though she was adopted and Susan was her real child. She had said she thought it might be because Jen was disabled, and had come from another country, so her mum was very protective.

'Did you mention Romania?'

'No, I dunno, I might have, anyway it wasn't Romania, it was Liverpool wasn't it? It's just that there was this bloke, a care worker, I think he fancied me, we used to have ciggies together on the balcony, he was from somewhere kind of that direction and he asked me lots of questions, like how much she knew about her background, so it did make me wonder.'

Susan wandered round the shelves looking at the titles and asking how he decided where to put things and how he knew what price to ask. 'Are you thinking of going into competition with me?' Bill joked.

'I was wondering if I could help here?'

'It doesn't really run to an assistant,' Bill said.

'No not for pay I'm on job seekers.' And as it still felt comfortable Bill said she could do a few hours perhaps. And he could give her something for minding the shop when he went to auctions.

'Do you think I should try and find the guy I talked to in rehab?' Bill was already wondering if he should be getting involved with Susan, he had seen how she could manipulate first hand in her dealings with Jennifer.

'No, best not,' he said.

5

It was not as though Boian were used to luxury, his mother had worked at the factory to keep food on the table, yet the poverty of his father's house shocked him as he stood alone in the place his father had called home for nearly thirty years. It was a wooden building, the last in a row of outhouses tacked on to the back of a house owned by the farmer who employed him. His neighbours, visible through the badly spaced planks, were two black cows and the horse he had used to work the fields. Boian had come at the farmer's request to remove his father's things. The bed in the corner was crumpled and dirty; he probably slept in his clothes straight from the fields. There was a chest with a broken lid, which served as a table, the empty bottle of beer on it seemed a testament to his loneliness. There were some shelves and an arm chair, it wouldn't take long to clear; he'd make a bonfire. Boian began to carry the larger items out to the back garden feeling resentful that Emile wasn't there to help. Emile had never visited, never seen his father after he had left, not till he was in a box, the village women said, they said it was because he loved his mother so much but according to Boian, he had no heart, he was a selfish pig.

He put the few cooking utensils in a box with some small tools and some other things that might be useful. People were poor, they were meant to be better off after Ceauşescu, but they weren't, not in the country anyway. In an old yellow tobacco tin he found three photographs, one a wedding couple; he recognised his mother, hopeful, in her white gown and veil, did they love each other then? *Paul and Dana, March 1968* was written on the back. Another photo', of him and his brother aged two and three, on the garden bench, lots of family, people he knew but so much younger. The last one, was of a christening, outside the church, he recognised himself and Emile and his mother holding a baby who was waving its arms in the sunshine. He stared at the last one, stuck in a deep sadness, the family that never was, at what his father had done, and at what he had lost, before the significance of the baby's waving confused him, embarrassed him, as though he'd been caught lying by his teacher.

He put the photo's quickly back in the box and onto the window ledge where he'd found them. Outside he took an axe to the chest and broken chairs, he was strong, he ripped and splintered the planks and piled the wood on top of the stuffing from the one armchair and lit it. It blazed immediately, sparks crackling off into the white hot sky. He fetched the bedding, the few clothes and work boots and threw them on, the smoke turned black and stank. The house was now empty, his inheritance polluting the countryside, and an old tobacco tin burning his conscience. He didn't leave immediately, he sat on a bench, watching the fire, rolling cigarette after cigarette. All the houses had similar benches, it was where the women would sit and clean the vegetables and gossip, it was on such a bench that the photograph of himself and Emile had been taken. In the picture he was bigger and rounder than Emile, even though he was the younger, but Emile could run, oh he could run, Boian had a memory of chasing him through the village with an axe, perhaps this same one now at his feet, determined on revenge for some merciless teasing, lucky Emile could run. Lucky Emile.

He went back into the house, took the tin from the ledge and went outside. He looked again at the photo's one by one, two of them he threw in the fire, watched them curl in the red charcoal and threw the tin after them, the third he put in his pocket, and left the property.

He walked through the village and out the other side following the bank of the river. Up above him was the sound of sawing as the ground was cleared in preparation for the building of houses for those who seemed to know how to work this new market system, like Emile perhaps. The river banks were clogged with the detritus of modern life. On the edge of the village the river had a natural bathing place, he and the other children had often played there. It was deserted, not so many children in the village now, and school was on. He stripped and went in through the plastic bags, squash bottles and plastic crates, to the centre and let himself float, like a piece of human pollution, in the flow of the river.

Emile ordered espresso, in his usual cafe by the river, inhaled his first smoke of the day and checked messages on his phone, nothing from Jennifer. She'd decided to stay with her English name, and Emile liked the Englishness of his business partner. No problem, he would call her later. He had half an hour before his meeting with the architect at the factory, then he must source the new machines, Russian maybe? Probably Chinese would be better; Jennifer would need to see all comparatives. Meanwhile he was behind on orders for home consumption, Jennifer wanted to develop the internal market, whilst expanding internationally – the global market, he rolled the phrase several times through his mind.

He parked his Renault in the usual place and went into the factory where the din of sewing machines was deafening. He'd begun with two machines in his mother's apartment, after she'd died, now there were a dozen, and nothing would stop him. In the vestibule bolts of cotton prints were being unpacked and carried straight to the cutting room. He employed twelve machinists, two cutters and two general workers for porterage and maintenance. He would double, perhaps treble this. In his office Emile switched on his computer. Beata came in to say one machine was down and did he want to borrow a domestic one until it could be mended or replaced? He agreed, and saw through the window the right hand drive Range Rover pull in alongside his car. The pang of envy he was expecting didn't come. Instead he noticed the age of the car, the dent on the mudguard, and excitement gathered round his heart. Soon he would have something better.

Beata brought the two men coffee, Emile didn't mind if she overheard something, best to get a buzz going. He leaned back in his chair and talked expansively about his proposed developments, a second storey, double the capacity, showroom, meeting room, paved car park. He could feel the architect weighing the situation, thinking Emile had gone off the rails, wondering how it was to be financed. Emile chose his moment to say that the drawings with all their necessary surveys and permissions needed to be ready in four weeks to discuss with his English business partner who would be visiting then. They shook hands and Emile escorted him out to the car, chatting about mpg, four wheel drive and fuel injection.

Returning to the office, satisfied, there was a message on his phone from Boian asking to meet him this evening, in town. His mood dipped. Boian always made him feel guilty, whether or not there was present need; the free floating guilt quickly turned to anger and he always did or said something he regretted which started the guilt circle all over again. He wasn't sure where Boian fitted in his new fortune; it had been Boian's idea to try and find their sister, because of some rubbish about releasing his father's soul. He texted back that he'd meet him at eight in the café bar opposite the station.

When Boian arrived, parking his old truck on the street outside, Emile was already in the café. He was sitting at a table in the window and was talking on the 'phone. He waved. In the café Boian squeezed in opposite him. The waitress took his order for a beer and Emile mimed he would have another brandy whilst he continued to negotiate prices with a wholesaler. Boian stared through the window. On the opposite pavement a train passed, the lines were open to the road, on the other side of the lines, pavement and then the river, the same one as passed through their village but much wider here in town. Directly opposite the café was one of the two bridges that spanned the river. On the far bank the Carol Hotel was glistening with new paint, white and gold with wooden balconies and red tiled turrets needle thin, restored to its pre-communist glory days and waiting for all the tourists that were supposed to come. Next to it was the dilapidated casino building, wooden scaffolding held struts in place to keep it from total dereliction, signs swung from the cross bars to warn pedestrians that lumps might fall off and cause injury. It had been like that for the whole of Boian's lifetime. There were plans to restore it but it was owned by the church who, newly establishing their power, were opposed to gambling yet were holding out for a big payoff from a developer. He noticed an ancient couple on the bridge, dark faces, the man with head bowed, asleep maybe, on a bench with no back, leaned on a stick placed between his legs; gypsies selling flowers probably. They had a bucket with some bunches of dreary peonies drooping on their stems and the old woman was pressing posies of hedgerow flowers on passers-by.

Boian had seen them before around his village, maybe they lived there. The train pulled into a station further up, no more than a shelter indicating the stop. People from the train were walking home, or into town, past the café window, carrying bags, everyone carried plastic bags. Emile continued to talk taking no notice of his brother. Abruptly the call finished, the brothers clasped hands and awkwardly hugged across the table.

'How are you man? It's good to see you. Sorry about that, no one seems to keep office hours any more. How's life? Still driving that old truck I see.'

'Yeah, well it goes.'

'Have to do something about that.'

Boian was wary, he wanted a new start with his brother, now they were alone, orphans; he wanted them to operate as equals and he knew he had to overcome this resentful little boy. But he was angry already; at Emile talking on the phone about the business that was more important than he was; about the way he connected his status to an old truck.

He needed to clear the air, get things straight. He would ask him how he had discovered Jennifer. Maybe he would show him the photograph.

Emile was high with new market adrenalin. 'I want you to come in with me man; it's really gonna be big, the architect was in today, there is huge potential for the site, and the orders we already got are good but with what Jennifer brings, man we're going global. You want to eat?' Boian shook his head 'Yeah, global man,' Boian said nothing. 'I'm building a new house on the forest side for Merta and the kids. You are my brother, you don't need to do deliveries for old skin flint Müller any more. I want you to be sales manager on the domestic side.'

'I don't know anything about that kind of work.'

'No problem, you'll have an office, new car, secretary, she'll arrange all your appointments you just have to charm the bollocks off the customers, can't say you're not good at that!' Boian didn't think he did have that particular talent. 'Real family business see. The three of us.'

'Have you heard from Jennifer?'

'Yeah, yeah, we're constantly in touch.' A pang of jealousy

tightened Boian's chest.

'Well what do you say?'

'I'll think about it.'

'Think about it? Lets drink to it man.' Emile downed his brandy. 'Gotta rush now, some young ladies at the Carol!' He got up and pocketed his phone. He pointed a finger at his brother 'Don't think for too long.'

'I cleared dad's stuff.'

'That's good. Don't suppose there was much, it's all yours anyway, I'll be in touch.' And he was gone.

Boian was incensed, the hairs on his body stood up like hackles on a dog's back, he would have snarled except his jaw was clamped shut and no breath reached his lungs.

The old flower seller came into the cafe and ordered two coffees from the counter. Boian took breath and called the waitress for brandy. Clutching her coffee the old woman made for the door, and waited expectant. Boian swivelled in his seat to open it for her.

'Seen you with your brother,' she said, 'and the lost one; best be wary.'

Stupid old bitch he said under his breath, what does she know of our business? He downed his brandy and left.

6

Jennifer caught the bus at the Angel. It had been a very good week, an excellent week; she had found possible backers and the business plan was shaping up. Why then was she not joyful, something felt odd? The bus was crowded, she navigated herself past the shopping trolleys and buggies. She finally got a seat and closed her eyes, she would doze up the Essex Road. Friday night she and Bill usually ended the week in a Turkish restaurant in Dalston. Of course, that was what was odd; being alone, or the prospect of it, Bill hadn't actually gone yet. She didn't feel so angry now, everything had been going at such a speed she had not thought about him. A little panic set in, they had been a good couple, for eight years, a long time, and buying a place together is a commitment. Well she'd bought it, but they'd chosen everything together. She wondered if he would demand half, they weren't married but he might have rights. She'd heard of cases. How ridiculous Bill wasn't like that. He'd cried when she'd asked him, told him, to go, his face screwed up in anger and pain, declaring his love, it was hard to bear.

A young mother struggled with a buggy manoeuvring it into the space in front of her seat, an older child sat next to her eating a bag of crisps. Bill had indicated early on that he would have liked children, Jennifer had made it quite clear they were not in her life plan and he hadn't mentioned it again. Lots of her college friends had got babies and toddlers and she was happy for them but it was not what she wanted. Well Bill could find someone and have his babies now, his clock wasn't ticking.

Maybe she would suggest they go out to eat tonight, just to sort a few things out, to be civilised, considering this she shocked herself with the thought that maybe they didn't have to split up. The child next to her on the bus stared, she must have gasped. She had been so convinced, so independent, so angry; yet considering now, whatever he had been doing in Macclesfield and for whatever motive, it was not to hurt her. She knew he wouldn't do that. And Susan; she hadn't called Susan, it had been two weeks and she'd deleted all her messages without reading them. What if she'd gone back on the booze? It would be her fault. She clamped her teeth together, she did not want dependents.

They'd reached Balls Pond Road. The mother expertly backed her buggy off the bus with one hand, holding her older child with the other. Next stop Newington Green.

On her way home from the bus stop she phoned *Mangal's* and booked a table, they would go out. He had gone to work for the last two days so he must be over the 'flu. There were no lights on in the house, but it was only just dusk. The front door closed behind her, there was no bike in the hall. She called, 'Up? Down?' without expecting an answer. Still at work? Or popped to the shop? She put her head in the sitting room though she knew he wasn't there and then went down to the kitchen, no note. Why should there be? She would change out of her work clothes and maybe he'd be back by then. The bedroom was tidy, the bed made, he must have done that, his considerateness warmed her. She opened the wardrobe and her stomach fell. His side was empty. She sat on the bed and tried to breathe steadily, reasoning with herself that this was what she wanted.

Later, after eating a crust of old bread and some hard cheese she had found lurking in the fridge, while washing it down with several whiskies, she became engulfed with grief. She wailed shouting his name so loudly the neighbours would hear, though no one in her area would take any notice.

The whisky kept her awake. Alternately wet through with sweat and then freezing cold she thought she had caught his 'flu. Every thought opened its gob like a devouring monster and reason, pathetic reason, fought back only to find battalions of sickening thoughts waiting to pounce. Identity was the prize. She was shrivelling. She was no-one. The night was marked by the chiming clock downstairs. At four a.m. she was in the drift to unconsciousness, but was jerked awake again by the terrifying image of the hospital bed where she had seen the man supposed to be her father, and in the dream her brothers were manacling her to its iron rails.

At six-thirty that same morning Susan stood, getting wet in slight drizzle, at the back gate of The Priory. She knew the shifts changed at seven in the morning and seven in the evening, but she didn't even remember the name of the worker she wanted to find, Cornet kept coming to mind but she didn't trust it. Men and women went past her taking no notice, sometimes stopping in a group to chat to those coming out. Not in English but what language it was she didn't know. Some drove in, bringing others with them. She counted cigarette buts on the pavements and in the gutter, forty-nine; people stubbed their cigarettes as they went in and lit up immediately on getting out. The rain got heavier and umbrellas went up. She hadn't got one. As it went towards seven she had counted fifteen leaving and twenty-three going in, perhaps they needed more staff in the daytime. None of them reminded her of Cornet, or whatever he was called. She stayed till quarter past and then wandered round to the front. Glistening white with battlements and arched windows radiating luxury, inside she knew it was total beige, nothing to get your teeth into, just superior do-gooders and blank walls with insipid pictures; yet she felt bad thinking this way, Jennifer had forked out a hell of a lot for her. She'd have been better off in Holloway. Well where was bloody Cornet then? Perhaps he'd left, they must come and go all the time.

She walked towards Roehampton, avoiding puddles and counting her steps in groups of fifty. Then the end came off one of the high heels on her boots and made a lower strike than the other; odd numbers left, sharp and high, metal on stone; even numbers right, dull, plastic. She went in the first café she came to and ordered a latte and some toast. The windows were steamed up but she sat looking out anyway, she hadn't thought beyond this time. She'd imagined finding Cornetto or whatever he called himself and him telling her all about the crooks that were extorting money off her sister, and she would be able to put everything right. The waitress came over and put her order in front of her. 'Thank you. Where are you from?' She blurted out.

'I from Romania.'

'Oh wow! I am trying to find someone from Romania.'

'Will I do?'

'No, no, a particular person, a man.' Susan explained that she had a Romanian friend who worked at The Priory and she had lost touch with him.

'What his name?'

'I call him Cornet,' she said hesitantly.

'Never heard that name. Those people at that table work at The Priory, maybe they know him?' Susan turned round and saw a group of three men and a woman having a cooked breakfast.

'Thanks, I'll ask.' The waitress went back and Susan drank some coffee. The group were chattering loudly in a foreign language.

'Excuse me.' They all looked at her. 'I am trying to find my friend, I have lost his number, he works at the Priory.'

'What's his name?' the woman asked.

'Cornet.' They looked blank and shook their heads.

'He was there a month ago, tall, over six foot, black curly hair, smoked a lot.'

'Do you mean Corneliu?'

'Yes yes, that's him, I called him Cornet.'

'He's gone.'

'Gone where?'

'Back home, probably trouble with his wife, won't I do darling, I'm not married?'

'Yes you are you pig,' said the woman. 'He might come back, you want to leave a message?'

Susan rummaged in her bag, found an envelope, the waitress who was keen to hear what was going on, lent her a biro. She didn't know how to spell Cornelliu. Fuck it. She wrote, *please call me, I am Susan, we smoked on the balcony, I need to ask you something* and added her mobile number. She folded it small and gave it to the woman whom she knew would read it, and probably throw it away, fuck it. She paid and got out fast.

It had stopped raining, tap thud went her boots as she counted her steps to the bus stop. She was a long way from home and the demons were snapping. She would catch a bus into town and just ride for a while. She felt safe on a bus, people on buses were far more accepting than those on trains; on trains they looked at you and looked away quickly, expert at never catching an eye. On busses they would talk. There was a young black guy and his daughter on the back seat, she joined them and felt comfortable. She even had a small sense of satisfaction for what she had attempted if not achieved, and Cornet, the name stuck, might call.

The young man and his daughter got off in Kennington and Susan waved bye-bye to the little girl. There was contact, it was getting better. At The Elephant she got off, there was a mall of cheap shops where her small confidence took her in search of new boots. The sun was out drying the streets, and the concrete tubs on the pavements were full of tiny daffodils, and crisp packets. Plenty of people about. She bought new boots with credit, now odd and evens had the same sound, she stuffed her old pair in a bin, and felt good as she walked towards Waterloo.

She stood on the bridge watching the Thames; her friends would be in Camden, she could walk there and find them. Drinking mates, the booze was the glue, they weren't real friends like other people had. Her phone chimed, over excited, she fumbled amongst the necessary safety charms of her handbag, maybe Cornet? Her fumbling switched it off; missed call alert. Fuck. Then a text alert, she pressed to read it. *Hi where R U? Do you want to meet up? Jen x* Susan pressed Jennifer's number and listened to it ringing, counting, she knew it was eight rings before the message cut in, please pick up; she did. Jennifer asked where she was, 'Just popped out, I've got nothing on, I can come over anytime, or meet you somewhere.' Jennifer said she should come to the house around lunch. 'Great, see ya.'

Jennifer was thankful that Susan sounded OK, she was up and out at ten o'clock in the morning. She imagined her buying milk and a newspaper, some bread, a normal routine. She lay back again in bed and was immediately asleep. Heavy sleep; dreaming of getting up; fighting to get up and failing. An insistent ringing, she was running away from a fire, then into consciousness and Susan shouting through the letterbox, 'Jen, Jen are you in there?'

In the kitchen, Susan sitting where she always sat, by the window, she'd been there on the welcome home dinner from the Priory, when Jen had first told them about Romania, and there again when Bill had returned with his news from Macclesfield. In the small, unloved garden a neighbour's cat was shitting in the flower bed, she banged on the window.

'I'm going to get it paved,' said Jennifer.

'They'll shit in the window boxes then,' they laughed.

'Why don't you get a cat, a big bruiser like Boris? He'll chase the others off.'

'I go away too often.'

'I'd come and look after it.'

They were on dangerous territory on two counts, where would Jen be travelling to so often? Was Susan responsible enough to have a house key?

'Why did we call him Boris?'

'Boris Karloff?'

'Bill and I have split up. He's left.'

Susan hesitated, she probably shouldn't say that she knew, anyway she didn't know, not that he'd physically gone.

'You don't seem very surprised?'

'When you didn't answer my messages I called him, he said you'd had a big row. He said you wanted him to go.' She was pleased with the plausibility of her answer, almost true, the best sort of lies.

'I don't know what the fuck I want, it's all got so fucking complicated.'

Susan said nothing. They sat across the table, Jennifer red eyed in pyjamas, Susan uncomfortable in new boots that were rubbing her ankles, both clutching mugs of coffee. The sun lit up the plane tree at the end of the garden. The whisky glass, and stale bread and cheese in front of them, and thirty odd years of knowledge behind them; knowledge which only made them more silent with each other.

'Maybe I should get a cat,' Jennifer said. 'Do you remember when we got Boris and he walked in as though he owned the place and was checking out the staff? I went with Dad to get him from the pet shop, he was meant to be for you, your cat, for your fifth birthday.'

'Dad chose his name of course, took him over, he really loved him, gave him much more affection than he gave us.'

'Boris loved us though . . .'

'Slept on our beds if we were ill . . .'

'Be at the front door when we came home from school; I was at college when he died.'

'Dad didn't cry, I thought he would.'

7

Boian arrived home after his day's deliveries, and parked his truck at the back of his apartment building. The evening was cold and damp, the sun never looked into this area surrounded as it was on three sides by the six storey block. One wing, now abandoned, had shutters rotting on their hinges, and the window glass shattered by the missiles of the village lads. Curtains left by former tenants hung in strips.

He locked his cab and walked round to the front of the occupied section. He passed the cubby hole where, in the not so distant past, the concierge would to sit to spy and report on the residents; it was empty now. The steps up to his flat on the third floor echoed with his history. His apartment was on a corner of the third floor, his mother had been given it when she began work at the factory, the village authority took it over when the factory closed, nothing ever got repaired. He'd made no changes since his mother died, it was comfortable, cold sometimes, but he could fix most things. The glassed in balcony filtered the evening light through the dirt streaks. From the window that faced the village he could see that the shop was open, he needed cigarettes.

Ana ran the shop and pleased herself when she opened. There was an old woman, surely the same old woman, the flower seller from the bridge, sitting on a bench outside the shop. Boian tried to remember exactly what had she said to him in the café? Told him to be careful? What did she know about his family? In a village everybody knows everything, only he didn't, and the photograph troubled his conscience; had Emile pulled off a scam? He wouldn't put much past Emile. Mother had told them their father had sold the child, and run off with the money. The orphanages were full in those days, and westerners wanted babies to adopt. Another story he'd heard was that the baby was crippled and sickly and wouldn't feed, his mother didn't want it, had never wanted it but had left it too late to get rid of it. Some said the disfigurement was because of her attempts to do so. He heard these stories and got on with his life. He had no memory of his sister, he remembered visiting the hospital to see his mum, the same hospital where his father had recently died, lots of babies crying, he had hugged his mummy but there was no tiny thing wrapped up in a cradle by her bed like there was by the others. When they had left, walking down the long red tiled corridor, he had heard a terrible scream, he had clutched his grandma who had soothed him and had said another little soul had come to vex us. Then there was the memory contained in the christening photograph.

The T.V. news was on but only because he liked the buzz; it was all rubbish, what the masses were allowed to hear, and some of their petty complaints, a gutter not mended or a block needing new windows. His phone registered a message; Emile asking him to call; he could wait. Somewhere his mother had a box of photographs, he'd played with them as a child; Snap and Happy families. Amongst baskets of buttons, half embroidered cloths, tins holding fasteners and tins holding pins, bits of lace, a pile of socks waiting to be darned for the last five years, there it was; an old brown tin that had once held sweets and had a barely distinguishable bunch of flowers embossed on the lid. He ate quickly. An hour passed, Emile called again and was ignored as Boian went through every picture in the box. There were studio photographs of his parents wedding, like the one in the other tin, photo's of the christening of cousins and second cousins; lots of him and Emile from babies up to about ten, no other child connected to his parents. He returned them to the box, put it back where he had found it and went out.

The old woman was no longer outside the shop, instead there was a gang of lads drinking lager. From his childhood he knew Ana, and her mother who sat all day in the back room watching television wearing a fur coat. He bought cigarettes from the sour faced Ana and asked her about the old woman on the bench. Ana's father had been killed after the revolution, he had been a government informer, and revenge had been taken by dragging him though the village behind a car. Boian was sixteen at the time and had cheered with the rest, now he was ashamed and always tried to be friendly and respectful to Ana. He had slept with her once after a village party, she didn't encourage it again and he didn't mind. She said she'd noticed the old woman, she'd seen her before but didn't know who she was, and in any case she could do without her sort hanging round.

He crossed the potholed road avoiding the drinkers, and sat on a concrete block to smoke. The ruins of the factory stretched from where he sat for about half a mile out of the village, his apartment block had been built to house the workers, his mother had been employed there, but since eighty-nine it had been slowly wound down and been left to rot. Many of the workers who had arrived with it had now left, gone back to their villages and the land. The building had long since been looted of every scrap of saleable material; it was an ugly monument to an ugly era.

He finished his cigarette and walked round the exterior, echoes of his childhood were all around. There had been good games in the factory yard. Now coarse grass and thistles grew over and between concrete blocks and rubble. The blackthorn was in blossom and the wind blew white petals like confetti, incongruous on his shoulders and dark hair. He followed a badger track and saw a small building, relatively intact up ahead, one storey with a smoking chimney. He wondered if this was where the old woman lived. A dog rushed forward, barking, reached the end of his chain and reared up. Boian's phone bleeped in his pocket; it was Emile saying he was at the apartment. He looked up at the snarling dog, and an old woman, it was her all right, came out to see what was up. 'What do you want?'

'I want to talk to you,' he shouted above the dog.

'I've nothing to say to you. Get off home.'

'You said something in the cafe. You told me to be careful. Of what?'

'Just be careful. Now get away from here.' Somebody shouted from inside the dwelling, she turned and went back in slamming the door behind her.

Boian retraced his steps. When he got home Emile was on the sofa.

'How d'you get in?'

'It was open.' Boian knew it wasn't.

'Where were you?'

'Just went out for ciggies, want a beer?' He fetched a couple from the fridge. 'Bit warm, the fridge is on the blink.'

'Have you thought anymore about my proposition?' Emile was nervy, his eyes darted everywhere, his fingers drummed on the beer can. This was not the reason for his visit.

'How did you find Janufa? I mean in the first place?'

'I told you there's a website that helps you search for relatives.'

'You mean you just put in Janufa, Romania, withered arm, and up she pops?'

'I don't know exactly, I paid an agency that does these searches, what's your problem?'

'I think we should check.'

'What do you mean?'

'DNA.'

'Sure, when she's next here. But it's her all right.' Emile, went to the window. 'Do you still see Ana?'

'No.'

'Merta's left me, taken the boys.' Silence, both men reflecting on history repeating itself. 'And I've had a break-in at the factory. Look man, we're family. I need you on my side. Will you come in with me? I've got to get better security and I don't know who to trust, there are all sorts of scum around.'

It was dark outside now, and the dogs had started their night calls. Occasional vehicles hitting the deep trenched road added another sound to the chorus. The T.V. from the upstairs flat was blaring, and young lads racing round the courtyard on mopeds and bicycles were shouting obscenities at each other, or yelling at passing women. Boian switched on a lamp and fetched brandy. He felt responsible, as though he were the elder and he needed to care for his brother; if there was trouble they could deal with it, as they'd faced off the village bullies all their childhood. Sure Emile had gone off the rails, but he'd got back on them again, and created his factory from nothing, just a few old machines in some sheds. The bottle went down. If Merta didn't want him Boian offered the spare room. The barking moved into howling and the moon rose above the factory like a German Romantic painting; the bottle was replaced and for the hours that were left before amnesia, they were brothers in league against the world.

At six a.m. Emile took a call. There was not much left of the factory when he arrived. The firemen had done a good job; they were coiling their hoses back onto the ancient engine. The few onlookers held their scarves over their faces and moved away from the stinking pile as Emile's Renault turned onto the forecourt.

8

It was ten a.m. when Susan turned the shop sign to 'Open' and picked up the post. She was 'in charge', proud and nervous, even though Bill had said that on a Monday there would be hardly any customers, and that she should sit and read for the day. Susan did read, very occasionally, the latest bestseller. The shop was dim and smelt of books, she sneezed, twelve times, paper always made her sneeze.

Putting the paperbacks out on the pavement she chatted with a couple of workmen on their way to Cosima's for breakfast. She took her time placing the books, deciding first on an alphabetical arrangement, then changing her mind and going for colour coding of jacket covers. Lots of orange, green and yellow, the mixed colours bothered her, for those that refused to fit she settled on mingling them in a separate tray.

Inside she noticed that the books were in different sections, archaeology, ancient history, biography. The alphabetical listing of authors gave an uneven look to the shelves and she would have liked to start again size and colour coding. She needed something to do; she made coffee and cleaned the surfaces in the little kitchen at the back, then emptied the cupboard, and cleaned all the shelves, throwing away outdated coffee, pickles and marmite, and bleaching the coffee stains from the mugs. The little fridge came up smelling fresh with its white interior gleaming, and she still had the challenge of the floor ahead. Would Bill be pleased? Would he notice, or worse would he think of her as a cleaner with no intellectual resources? Well perhaps she had none, she tried to remember the last book she'd read, Captain somebody's mandolin, but she couldn't remember anything about it. She'd not been to the cinema in six months, let alone the theatre. Jennifer and Bill went to the theatre often, she had heard them discuss plays. She scrubbed and rinsed determined to read when she had finished, then the shop door went: fuck! What did she look like? Maybe if she didn't appear they'd go away, but what if they stole a book? Would Bill miss it? He couldn't know all the stock, it would be listed, but would he check when he got back? That would be a stock take – a stock take – she liked that thought, something she could do for him, checking each book against his lists . . .

'Hello . . .' Susan stayed still. She could hear some movement out there and the ticking of a small clock on the wall next to her.

'Just a minute.' She heard herself say in a tiny voice. Handbag to check make-up. Damn her bag was on the counter. She counted breaths as she had been taught.

The customer was just leaving as Susan put her head through; she'd been seen. 'I thought there was no-one here.'

'I was busy in the back.' Damn she'll think I was on the lavatory. The customer was a woman late fifties, expensive hair-cut, lovely cardigan. 'Can I help at all, I'm just minding the shop for the owner, he's away today.'

'For Bill?' Christ she knows him.

'He was looking for some early translations of Chekov for me, I can't be doing with these 'versions' they do now.' Susan had no idea what she meant. 'Is he back soon?'

'Tomorrow.'

'Tell him I'll call in later in the week. Bye now.'

Susan felt pathetic. She should have engaged with the woman, said, 'Good morning . . ., can I help?. . Let's check the shelves . . . let me look in the back for new arrivals . . . sorry, can you come back? I'll leave a note for Bill.' Instead she'll come back and say she spoke to the cleaner.

You were not supposed to indulge in self-criticism she'd learnt at *The Priory* from those who had never had anything to criticise themselves about. Determinedly she found the drama section and some books by Chekov. *Russian playwright and short story writer, born in Taganrog in southern Russia in 1860.* She pulled out a book of short stories and settled in an easy chair that Bill had squashed in a corner for his customers and began to read. The whole thing was thirty-two pages. She would read six. It was so old fashioned. She struggled on, despite being hungry and needing coffee. Her mind wandered, there was a pub down the road, in both directions, and one opposite. Could she trust herself to go to the café?

She pulled the blind down on the door and turned the sign to closed. It was a fine morning she could leave the books outside.

The workers she'd talked to earlier were sitting at a table outside Cosima's, smoking. She brought her coffee out and joined them; they nodded at her. 'Hello. Not many customers, thought I'd have breakfast.' They looked at her, 'I'm from the bookshop.' They smiled across at her.

She lit a cigarette and stubbed it out again as her bacon sandwich arrived. The day was quite cool. April was like that, it never knew what season it wanted to belong to. People passed by, a woman with a pushchair full of washing heading for the laundrette. A couple of community police, their pockets bulging with technology, strolling importantly. Busses growled by, a scaffolding lorry opposite caused the traffic to build up in both directions. Young men threw the poles between them as if they were made of balsa. Poles from the Poles was written on the side of their lorry. She clasped both hands round her mug of coffee, she was shivering now. The workmen had left and the two police had taken their place. She smiled at them.

'Haven't seen you before?' the police woman said.

'I'm from the bookshop.'

'Bills place?' Why couldn't they mind their own, what the fuck business was it of theirs?

'Yes, he's gone to a sale in Bristol.'

'Didn't know he had an assistant.' Well you fucking know now Susan would have liked to have said. She didn't like the police.

She made a detour on her way back through a little dog-shit park. A group was clustered round a bench with their special brew, their dogs racing round them, scrapping among themselves and chasing any passing pedigree. She vaguely recognised one of them from her Camden pub.

She felt much better by the time she was back in the shop. She needn't tell Bill she had been out so long, he'd said there'd probably be no customers. She'd text him and say all was going well, and mention the Chekov, she'd take control. She waited anxiously for the chime of a message in reply, none came, perhaps he was driving. She settled back in the armchair and picked up *The lady with the lap dog* again, old fashioned bloke after a bit of high class totty, footballers wives was more fun. Still, if she didn't like the book she liked the fact she was reading the book. It was part of her convincing 'proper person' behaviour.

Her phone chimed a message, Bill, she thought immediately but there was no name, a number she didn't know at the top. She pressed to read. *Dear Susan how can I help you Corneliu.* She pressed the call return it went straight to voice mail, she spoke, *Hi, Susan here, got your text, really kind of you, want to ask you some things – about Romania, thinking of going there for a holiday. What are you up to? Could we meet up or something?* She sat and waited, steadied her breathing, nothing. She couldn't concentrate on the book, she wandered the shelves clutching the phone. She stared out of the window, the Poles had finished the scaffolding and were driving away. The phone chimed, and the text read *sure thing, 5pm? Where shall I meet you? C.* Susan texted back, *I'm at work* and gave the address.

Like a fourteen year old on a first date Susan prepared immaculately; as Corneliu opened the shop door she was on a stool behind the counter with her Chekov opened before her. Corneliu was over six feet, slim, stooped with black curly hair, in jeans and a denim jacket, Adidas trainers. 'Hi darling, how are you, good job eh? You like reading yes? Ah Chekov, I like Three Sisters.'

'What? No, one sister, Jennifer, I told you.'

'No Chekov play, *The Three Sisters,* Olga, Masha, Irena!'

'Of course,' she covered her mistake with a laugh.

'Have you finished? Shall we go for a drink? I help you with your holiday.' Together they carried the trays of paperbacks into the shop chatting about the books and authors unknown to Susan. 'We go to pub yes?'

'Yes sure, orange juice for me.'

The Rose and Crown on Caledonian Road was a drinking pub old style, nothing scrubbed or gastro, just men drinking pints and a few dry sausage rolls in a plastic cabinet. The girl behind the bar was chatting to a young man and paid them no attention. Susan had spent many days in places like this and never noticed the smell of stale beer, dirty carpets and disinfectant. She drank her orange juice quickly and bought another getting a second pint of bitter for big C. He liked being called Cornet and was pleased she had found him. He told her about his childhood in the north, how everyone was frightened and nobody trusted anybody. How he'd move to Bucharesti to get work and that even now it was difficult to get visas to leave. He'd been lucky to know someone at The Priory. They went outside to smoke, the pub got busier, the group from the park were at another table outside, their dogs tied underneath. It got cold, she bought Corneliu whisky, he was shocked at the price. 'Cheaper to buy from supermarket.'

'Sure but then we have nowhere to go.'

In the little park they sat close on a bench and Susan sipped her whisky from a paper cup.

The sun was setting behind him, as Bill drove along the Westway into London. He hadn't thought of Jennifer all day. The back of his Ford estate car was weighed down with boxes of books that he'd have to make space for. Some original stock could go, shelf fillers he'd bought at the start for next to nothing, and today he had sold his sports section to a specialist buyer, including *Taylor on Golf*. He would get Susan to help pack them up while he catalogued the new stock. He could see himself enjoying having an assistant. Perhaps he was dimly aware that helping Susan, trusting her, giving her a job, was a way of connecting to Jennifer.

His plan was to drive straight to the shop, maybe picking up a burger on the way. He drove all the way along the Marylebone Road from Lissom Grove to King's Cross without having to stop for one red light. Great, he'd go straight to the shop and eat later.

A space to park outside was another bit of luck. He was pleased to see the shop was all closed up properly, blinds down, no trays left outside. He knew she'd been there because of her text. She'd have to learn not to text him every time there was a customer. He piled the boxes up on the pavement and opened the door. The top security lock was open. He'd have to tell her about that. Not that he thought his stock was interesting to the local burglars, but kids could make such a mess just for fun. He dragged the last box in. There was a smell of cigarettes, bloody Susan, he'd have to tell her about that too. The boxes could stay where they were till morning, he was knackered.

There was a noise from the back room, something falling and

rolling. Seconds passed with a rush of ridiculous thoughts; a cat had got in; a window left open; the wind; junkies; someone wanted to murder him. Another noise soft and sibilant. Someone was in there. Oh God! A minute passed of silence. Another minute went by and he knew he had to look.

He opened the door fast, something – a bottle – rolled away as he snapped the light on. The table had been pushed against the sink, a pile of his dust-sheets and an old duvet had been pulled from the cupboard and onto the floor; Susan lay under the duvet with a dark haired man next to her. Bill stooped and retrieved the empty bottle of whisky. 'Get out.'

'This is Cornet Bill, from Romania, he used to work at the Priory.'

'Get out now.' And then, because he was a gentleman, Bill went back into the shop. He could hear them rustling and rummaging and dragging the table back. After five minutes they came out, Corneliu first. He said nothing.

'I'll come back and clear it all up in the morning,' Susan said.

'Don't come back, ever!'

9

The children traipsed obediently after Dana, she said they were to be good and left them at her mother's gate; she avoided the lecture that way. She'd been in the fields all day, picking beetroot, the first of the season from winter sowing. She walked slowly, not from tiredness, she was strong and life had taught her not to complain, she went slowly because she could see that Olga was not waiting by the bus stop as they'd agreed. It wasn't good to be seen hanging round, people were nosey, stories got told. There was a seat near the stop so she sat down, she'd look as though she were waiting for a bus, although she knew the last, the only, bus had gone hours ago. She pulled her headscarf forward on her face. There was no one about anyway. In the field behind her an old horse came slowly over and put its head over the fence. It should have gone to the canning factory long ago. Its owner must be sentimental; they must have plenty to eat she thought; perhaps they work for the secret police. She admonished herself for her chain of thought. A horse puts its head over a fence and she is already in prison, for what? It's not against the law to wait for a friend. It was after six now and she was beginning to think of going home when a truck pulled up opposite and Olga got out. It was not what they'd arranged, they were going to meet by chance, now her husband knew, what did he know? 'Dimitru is taking feed round to his cousins so I grabbed a lift.' Dana was shocked at this carelessness. 'What's the matter? Don't you feel well?' Olga asked.

'I'm fine shall we walk?' They set off together along a track used to take the carts into the fields. Olga was the older, at forty she was middle aged, with grey hair and coarse skin, and fat, not the fat of good living, but of bad food and tired muscles. Dana would be like her too but at twenty-seven she could still wear the clothes she wore at twenty, which was just as well as there was no money for more.

After a little way Olga turned off into a field. 'I was working

in here last week and I noticed a good patch over in the corner.'
They kept to the edge as best they could, the field had been
planted with late potatoes, and soon their feet were heavy with
clay. 'Have you brought a trowel?' Olga asked.

'Oh! I forgot, have you got one?'

'It's you who want this, I just said I'd show you, that's all.'

'And tell me what to do?'

'Yes and we agreed fifty lei.'

'We can't go back.'

'Well you'll have to dig with your hands.' They reached the
corner where the horse drawn plough had left a patch unfur-
rowed. 'That's them.' Dana stared at the familiar weeds.

'Which ones?'

'Didn't they teach you anything in school?' Certainly not this
Dana thought. 'It's the one with the feathery leaves, sort of grey-
ish, just there, tons of it.' Dana stared, she knew some names,
dock, sorrel, ground elder, and this one Olga was referring to was
very familiar but she'd never known it was wormwood, or what it
could be used for. 'The roots go very deep, and you need to get it
out whole, you'd best find some stones to dig with.' Dana set
about her task, Olga sat where the bank rose a little and got out
some tobacco and rolled herself a smoke. Half an hour must
have past already and Dana would have to get back to the boys
before bedtime, and she didn't want to have to make up a story
for Paul. After about ten minutes, she was covered in mud but
had three whole roots which she wrapped in the newspaper that
she'd brought and pushed them to the bottom of her bag.

'How do I cook them?' Olga roared with laughter.

'You don't cook them, they wouldn't go up if they were soft!'
She roared again, asking for fifty lei through her wheezing.

'Don't I pay you after, when it's worked?'

'That's not what we agreed.' Dana couldn't waste time arguing,
she had the money ready.

'What do I do then?'

'Well, you put a bit of string round the top end and tie it to
the top of your leg, then you shove it up, right in and up as far as
you can go, or it won't work. Keep it in for a day or more if necessary, it'll do the trick, then you can pull it out and nobody the

wiser. You go back the way we came, I can walk to Dimitru's cousin's place over the field. Good luck.'

Her mother was not pleased, the boys had been fighting and Boian had wet himself. He was sulking now, wearing a pair of his grandma's knickers and being laughed at by Emile. Dana hurried them out apologising to her mother, and pulling her coat to hide her muddy trousers. At home she pushed her newspaper parcel to the back of the cupboard, and fought with a tired, angry Boian to get him in the sink. Emile fetched the sticks to feed the stove, and tickled up a flame, a big boy's job. Her husband was back already in the shed hiding three bags of potatoes and one of carrots under the woodpile so they would not be taken tomorrow for the collective; he would be fined or worse if they found them, but he'd got away with it before, and he knew that others did it. She boiled onions for the soup, added barley and cut up the loaf. She fed the boys, Boian, in his high chair was clean now, and calmer. It was dark before Paul came in. She put his meal on the table and tucked the boys up in their bunk and pulled the curtain across.

Later with the table cleared and the mattress down she crept up close to her husband, tired or not she had a plan, he was surprised and pleased, he rolled over her and kissed her roughly. She knew that tonight there could be no mistakes, too late for that; she relaxed and held him tight when he went to withdraw. Now she was safe, he wouldn't want her again for two days, she could do the business with the wormwood. As his snoring became regular she slid out of bed and took the parcel from the cupboard. Outside the night was clear, there was going to be a late frost, she could see the crystals forming on the crinkled edges of the cabbages by the back door. She pulled her coat over her nightdress; the moon shone in through the shed door as she opened her parcel. The roots were covered in earth, stupid she hadn't thought to clean them, she couldn't do it like that, she'd die of something else. She took one out to the animals' water tank and scrubbed it with her hands till they and the root were rough and raw. Back in the shed she attached a string and squatted down to do what Olga had described, she pushed as hard as she could and almost cried out with the pain. She hid the other two roots under the bench in a sack pile, Olga had said it might take two or three goes. Pleased to be back in the warmth of the bed, the pain eased, sometime, much later, she fell asleep.

When she woke, Paul was gone, Emile was pulling lumps from the loaf and Boian was crying by her head. 'He made me wet and he stinks', Emile said.

'It's a pity you can't see to him, and leave some of that bread for others.' She rolled gingerly out of bed. Everything in place, she dressed to begin the day. Emile would take himself to school. Boian would go with her.

Work had started when she arrived, that would be a black mark. Olga was there, they ignored each other. She went to her place, a small stool beside a mountain of beetroot. Taking a sack from a jumble by her feet she began to fill it from the heap that was as high as the barn roof. It was a sitting down job, she was lucky, last week she had been pulling up the roots out in the field. Boian played with some other children on the mud floor. 'Be sure to tell me if you want to go,' Dana said.

'Is he wetting again?' asked her neighbour, 'Ifan did that, but his father gave him the strap, that cured him.' Dana was afraid that Paul would have the same idea and tried to hide Boian's incontinence when she could, or else blamed herself for being too busy to see to him.

After the lunch break an official arrived and spoke to the foreman. They liked to throw their weight around, and watch women work. When they went into the office, the women gossiped with one another, pleased to have no one checking on them. Dana rested a while, 'You're getting behind, said her neighbour, we'll all be penalised.' At that point the two men came out of the office and Olga was called. Olga left with the official. The work continued, three to a mountain.

'Hey,' a woman shouted, 'we're one short.'

'Well you'll have to work harder then or stay late,' the foreman answered from behind his newspaper. The women worked on in silence, except for the rumble of root landslides.

When Paul returned from the fields that evening Dana told him what had happened. 'I'm not surprised, she's been asking for it.'

'What do you mean?'

'Not so many babies in the village as there used to be; they keep their eye on these things.'

They ate their supper in silence, Dana cleared the dishes and mended the children's clothes, the evenings were getting lighter now, there was more time for chores. Night came with a covering of cloud. 'Shall I pull the mattress down?' Paul asked. Dana was relieved the day was over.

Later in the shed, in total darkness she crouched to pull at the wormwood. There was no bleeding, her baby was staying put. She felt under the bench amongst the dirty sacks for the newspaper parcel which she threw with the naked root onto the compost heap as she returned to bed. Let the rats have it, she thought.

At work the next day, the remains of the beetroot mountains, reduced by yesterday's labour, still had to be bagged. It was eleven o'clock when the coach arrived and all eleven women were told to get in.

A policeman was shouting 'Leave the children', the women swearing, demanding, to no avail. The foreman joining in, worried about quotas, demanded their early return. Some women had a good idea what was going on, they had had dealings with Olga, perhaps they'd been denounced. Others, the louder ones, swore and complained out of youth and innocence. The coach jolted them along a dirt track for half an hour and then on a made up road to the outskirts of the city and a concrete building where they were left in a waiting area. A few women whispered together, most were silent. They were taken singly for questioning, Dana was near the front of the queue.

'Do you know Olga S?'

'Yes, I work with her.'

'We know that, what other dealing do you have with her?'

'None.'

'Then why were you walking in the fields with her two nights ago?' Shit they knew that.

'I was going to her cousins.'

'Going to her cousins?' And on and on and round and round. 'What were you digging?'

'Sorrel for the soup, horseradish for the sauce, potatoes for the pot.'

'Does your husband like horse radish? Does he like it hot? Do you like it stiff?' And on and on, and then alone, on the bench, hours passed.

In the medical room, strip, lie on the table, open your legs. So let them do a good job and dig out this foetus.

'You can dress now. Did you know you were pregnant?'

'No.'

'You liar, you waste our time.'

Dana was released and got a bus home, worrying about Boian, and how to explain to Paul. It was way past work time; she didn't know where the children would be. Home and Paul furious; 'Where have you been, who have you been with? . . Liar,' slap.

' Ask the others, you'll find out tomorrow,' slap, weeping, sobbing. 'Paul, I'm pregnant.'

10

Two fantastic meetings with high street fashion houses where against the odds, considering the economic climate, she'd secured the capital project funding for the factory. 'Wh-hey!' she said as she came in the door.

'It went well then?' Sally, her P.A. who knew everything, smiled at her and asked if she wanted anything else before she left.

'No you go now, I won't be long. I'll lock up. Have a good weekend.' Of course it would have to go to the lawyers, but in principle she was there. Final check of the inbox. Nine straight deletes, designer clothes, designer training, discount theatre, cheap airline tickets - save that one. A dinner invitation for her and Bill, friends from India; deal with it later, and the one she was looking for, subject *factory*. This would be Emile's initial report and costing, how brilliant would be her reply!

Dear Jennifer, Hope that you and your partner Bill are well. I am very sorry to tell you that things are not so good with me. My wife left me last week and took the children, she thinks I work too much and don't give them good time, but I work for them I tell her, and build a house for them, she says she will be just as lonely there.

Also, there has been accident at the factory, a fire three days ago and everything gone. You said maybe we build new factory so maybe not so bad. But workers have to go home, and orders cancelled.

Boian has not been much help to me, I haven't seen him since the fire, he doesn't answer his phone.

I look forward to hearing from you and wonder when you can come again to meet the architect?

Your loving brother, Emile.

Her heart no longer racing, slid down towards her belly. Was the ice cracking? Her credibility certainly would if this fell through after her presentations today. Once on a management training course the group was asked to walk around the classroom and select a partner by eye contact and mutual consent. It was one of those terrifying moments that she replayed over and over again; the fear was not that she wouldn't be chosen, but that she would be chosen by the wrong person.

She phoned Bill, 'How's things?' she wanted the familiarity and security of his voice.

'Oh you know, much the same, could do without your bloody sister.' His voice was harsh. Not helping.

'What has she done now?'

'You don't want to know. Why did you call?'

'Thought we might meet.' Silence on the other end, then Bill said OK. Jennifer suggested their usual Dalston café, and that was that.

Bill arrived first, and sat waiting with a beer. The pictures on the walls printed on fabric, were of rocky coves and fishing boats. Did they help the waiters feel less homesick? What would he have on the wall if he lived in Turkey, a London bus? A mural of the British Library? Jennifer was ten minutes late, an achievement for her, and, out of character, she apologised. The waiter greeted her as a regular, and she asked about his kids. 'How's the shop?' Jennifer asked, and regretted that her opening words should have been about work.

'Ticking over.' He wouldn't ask about her venture and she knew that.

'There's a leaking radiator in the spare room, I've had it fixed but we'll have to get the floor up and see if it's done any damage.' He heard *we'll have to* . . .

'I could come round on Sunday and have a look?'

'That would be brilliant,' then modifying her enthusiasm, 'anytime really, you've got a key. I'll probably have to go away next week.'

'Romania?'

She was agitated and launched, while their kebabs congealed on the plate, into a surge of words, a rush of all her fears and hopes and uncertainties; she told him the facts she knew, the fire, the family, and the doubts, the disquiet and uneasiness she felt. She was oblivious of his agenda, not understanding that her fear was a life jacket to him, that her uncertainties were oxygen to a drowning man, she went on and on and Bill only heard the spaces that he might slip into. She had to go out there, did he agree? He quite saw that, and the factory burning down was not a problem as she saw it, rebuilding was probably a better option than extending anyway. He wondered about possible sabotage, but agreed probably it was an accident. That suspicion was the prevailing culture was to be expected in a post-communist economy. Boian being missing worried her; he's a grown man Bill comforted, he can take a trip if he wants, you said he was not too fond of his brother.

They ordered a second bottle of Turkish wine, Jennifer stared through the window to a shop on the other side of the road; bride and groom in Kingsland Road glory, the groom's suit was cream with satin edging to the jacket, buses flickered the picture. Bill paid for the meal and they took the half empty bottle with them. In the next door shop they paused to stare at an enormous bed, curlicues of brass, layers of lace, with an integral television at the foot.

'I used to dream of a bed like that when I was little.' She said, astonishing Bill who knew her style to be minimal, floors bare, walls white, scarce a door handle visible. Bill said, 'we'll get one.' It was like the start of a relationship not the end. They ran for the bus, giggling like teenagers, missed it, and decided to walk. Back at the house they put Blossom Dearie on the CD player, finished the wine and Bill offered to come with her to Romania, and Jen thought it was a great idea, and later because neither of them could make a decision Bill fell asleep on the sofa, and Jen crept up to bed.

He had left by the time she got up, the note said, 'Gone to open the shop, see you Sunday Bx.' Saturday morning and she arrived at the office with her stomach lurching with nausea every few moments. She shut her office door and stared at the screen. There were decisions to be made.

On Sunday she woke to banging in the next room, grabbing a dressing gown she peeped in, she knew it would be Bill, he still had a key, and most of his possessions were in the house.

'You frightened me,' she said.

'Hi, didn't want to wake you.'

'That's why you were hammering?'

'Sorry.'

'Do you want some breakfast?' After her shower she cooked bacon and eggs. A Sunday routine when they were together. He washed his hands in the kitchen, as though it were his kitchen. She would have to sell, it was too painful.

'I've got a flight for Romania.'

'Great, when do we go?' Bill said.

'I just got one ticket.' She felt miserable saying it.

'Right.'

Into the silence she poured justifications; cuckoo she said as one egg rolled over the nest, cuckoo, as her egg was laid, and cuckoo she will say as she flies away.

'Strangely,' she said, 'the thing I'm most worried about is Bojan.'

'Stranger still,' Bill said 'to be missing a sister and a brother.'

'Do you mean Susan? What's up, I thought she was helping you?' and Bill took unrepentant pleasure in telling her about Susan and her latest conquest, and her return if not to the gutter, then to somewhere pretty close.

'I'd have thought you'd have been in touch?' Bill said, 'but of course she's not your sister. I'll leave the floorboards up so the joists can dry out. I don't feel like breakfast.' He picked up his bag of tools from the hall and was gone.

At mid-day, the tarmac shimmered and the heat tasted of metal. She had got a four hour journey ahead of her; she hired the only automatic car with air conditioning, her short arm didn't allow for changing gear. The airport was north of the city so she was soon on the A1 motorway, the sole decent road in the country. The landscape was flat, in every small town or collection of houses there were people selling by the roadside, vegetables, embroidered cloths, decorated wooden utensils. Women head-scarved against the heat, and old men in straw hats, sometimes selling from a cart with the horse still in the shafts, and it too with a sun hat. The dogs slept; the car purred through the miles. After a couple of hours the ground began to rise, she would be in Sinaia by mid-afternoon. She had decided to stop there and eat and probably phone Emile. She hadn't told him she was coming.

The marble entrance hall of the Palace Hotel was cool, she

went through to the lounge and ordered afternoon tea, English, and looked out over the unkempt park; grass and weeds over-grown and brown with the heat. The statues, reminders of former grandeur, looked on forlornly, they too dishevelled, and streaked with brown. They seemed as though they remembered when King Carol and his sad wife spent their summers in Peles Palace, up the hill, when carriage loads of guests would arrive at the casino in the park.

She listened to the 'phone ringing and ringing, which worried her slightly as she knew Emile was stitched to his mobile. Tea arrived, weak and tasteless, Liptons, with sandwiches of something pink her mother would have called luncheon meat and a cake with synthetic cream. Her phone rang; Emile showed on the screen. 'Hello, Jennifer. Good to hear from you.'

'I'm in Romania, in Sinaia actually, I'm aiming to reach Bistritsa by evening. I'll drive on in the early morning, can you book me into The Carol? Join me for dinner. All news then.'

'Wonderful that you are here.'

'Is Boian back?'

'He's probable holed up with some young lady! He'll turn up.'

'See you later.'

Back on the road, Mahler on the ipod, mountains and meadows to make her weep; buoyed up by hearing Emile's voice, she felt in control. She'd kicked her old support system in the face, Bill, Susan; funny to think of her dear wrecked sister as support. So now, in the moment and alone. Probably a good thing the factory burnt down, building anew would be easier. She would ask the questions and get the answers.

The bar was full of businessmen and young women. Jennifer could feel eyes on her and was relieved when Emile came through the swing doors; he hugged her, ordered drinks and acknowledged one or two of the other customers. A burly man, balding, forties, came up to talk. Jennifer was ignored in the usual way, she understood some words, the man seemed to be sympathising, about the fire she wondered, or was it Boian? Emile eventually introduced her as his business partner. The fat man grinned, disbelieving and moved away. Not a good start. Is there news of Boian? Jennifer asked immediately. Emile paused, 'Some rumours, nothing really, let's go to the dining room.'

The floor to ceiling windows would have given a view across the park but scaffolding, from which canvas sheeting was hung, totally covered the front wall. No work appeared to have progressed in the two months since her previous visit. The large dining room, where each table was laid with white linen, silver plated cutlery and heavy glass, was empty. Emile led her to one of the concealed windows and a young waitress appeared. Emile spoke to her for some time and when she left he said, it is best not to bother with the menu, it's a work of fiction anyway. The waitress brought two glasses of plum brandy, and a bottle of red wine. They were silent while she opened it and gave it to Emile to taste.

There was so much to say but neither of them was prepared to start; both wary of what they might discover. Jennifer recognised the playacting, the posturing, the big talker and minded none of those things. He liked business, as she did, they were similar, but not physically. She told him that the loss of the factory did not necessarily alter any of their plans. To build from scratch would cost very little more and the machines were obsolete anyway. The problem was his income whilst the business got started. He waved that away, big talk about other ventures.

The waitress returned with a plate of cold meats, Jennifer asked if Boian had spent time away like this before, and Emile evaded answering. He was a wild boy, always in trouble as a teenager, never settling down to work. Mother's favourite though, and the girls all liked him, but no prospect for a wife. It would be better when they were in business together. Jennifer hadn't realised. 'Oh yes, it's all fixed, he is going to be our domestic sales director.' Jennifer thought she should have been consulted on this.

'Well I hope not an absentee one. You mentioned rumours?'

'He has been looking into things that happened a long time ago; some people found ways round the system, everywhere there were informers; these things are best forgotten.'

The fat man waved goodbye from the bar. They remained the only diners.

'How does this place stay open with no business?'

'They are full in the winter season, and they pay rubbish

wages!'

'Do you think the fire at the factory and Boian's disappearance are connected?' Emile roared with laughter, perhaps a little too loudly. 'Have the insurance company looked into how the fire started?'

'The building was old, well you saw it, and there were lots of inflammable materials around, maybe a worker disobeyed and had a cigarette inside, maybe the electrics were dodgy, maybe just the hot weather.'

'Yes all those maybes, but we need to know, the insurers definitely will.'

'As you say, best to start with a clean sheet, best to do a new build, the fire was a favour really. Tomorrow we will visit the architect.'

'Was the building insured Emile?'

'Things are different in this country, we have to work with what we have, otherwise nothing would get moving and we would stay in this economic back woods forever. Yes I paid money, for insurance, but not quite like in England maybe.'

Jennifer was beginning to understand that this venture might not be as straightforward as she had imagined.

11

Cold sweat was trickling between Susan's breasts when she woke; she pressed her tee shirt against herself. The room was dim, the only light filtered through thin drawn curtains, hanging on a string and torn at the bottom. This was not where she lived; her heart thumping was drowning traffic noise, or else was the traffic noise; she was panicking, she pulled at her skin and her hair and bit herself till she could taste blood.

As her eyes adjusted to the light in the room she saw bottles reflected in a dressing table mirror, she half fell out of bed, to find they were empty. She lifted a vodka bottle to her lips, it was as dry as the inside of her mouth; she wretched, the woman in front of her wretched and she screamed, and screamed. The door flew open and someone came in and slapped her, 'Shut up bitch there are people trying to sleep'. Susan whimpered and the woman who had hit her relented, she continued in a foreign accent, 'You have to get out now. Corneliu only has the night time.' Susan's mind was clearing, she'd come here with Cornet. What did the woman mean? 'Get your things and go, go. Don't you understand English? Someone else takes the room now, come back tonight if you want, unless Corneliu brings another woman.' The woman laughed at this and started coughing. 'Five minutes', she spluttered, and left.

Susan dressed and found a lavatory. She was in a flat, doors to other rooms were shut. She could hear someone in a kitchen at the end of a corridor. She clutched her bag and counted her steps towards the noise. 'Hello.' A man, thirties maybe, balding, unshaven was making a cup of something. 'You want a cup of tea?' Same foreign accent, like Corneliu.

'Yes please.'

'You Corneliu's woman?' She supposed she was, 'I thought he must be with a woman, he hasn't been here for a while.' He passed her the tea and she held it not moving or drinking. 'Where is he?'

'God knows, I never see him.'

'Can you direct me to the tube station?'

'What do you mean?'

'I need to know where the underground is?'

'Don't think we have an underground in Parkeston darling.' Susan dropped her tea, the cup broke and the tea scalded her foot. She apologised and tried to pick up the pieces.

'Is she still here? Get her out Thomas.' The woman's voice from the corridor. Thomas got her a chair. 'You're in a state, sit down, do you not know where you are?'

'We came in the dark.'

'He's a bastard that man.'

'I have to get to London. I live there.' She felt for her purse in her bag, it was there, thank God. How much for a ticket to London. Thomas thought maybe fifteen or so pounds. 'I only have £7.43p.'

'Oh that's a good one.' Thomas said. Susan couldn't hold back tears.

'Get her out I said,' the voice from the corridor.

'It's OK Ma. Come on now.' Thomas took her under the arm and led her from the room. At the front door of the flat he said there was a bus stop opposite, then he shoved a fiver in her hand. 'That bastard had better pay me back,' she heard him say from the staircase.

Outside was a car park, she wandered, peering through windows trying to remember the car she'd arrived in with Cornet. It was hopeless, how she came to be in this town was a complete blank. She noticed a sign, Una Road, there were bus stops on both sides just where she emerged from the car park, but which way was the station? She needed to ask someone, but there was no one about: She was panicking badly, having difficulty breathing; must keep walking, and counting. She turned right, Garland Road, she must remember the names, came to a patch of green, the sign said 'Welfare Park' she found a bench, sat down and kept rigidly still for about twenty minutes. Counting, breathing. A group of beer drinkers were clustered round a bench not very far from where she was sitting. She worked out a sentence in her head, 'Excuse me please, could you please tell me how I can get to London?' she practised it for a while and then walked steadily she thought, over to the group.

She said her bit. 'You alright love?' Her breath was going again, 'Come here sit down,' she did. 'Have a drop of this.'

She took a swig of cider, 'Thank you.' The group, three men and a woman talked and laughed together. Susan felt calmer. 'Please can you tell me how to get to London?'

'Well there's a train from Harwich every hour, that's if you got twenty quid.' Her face must have answered because he said, 'Thought not, well best go down the docks and pick up a lift.' Susan was hyperventilating, 'Ease up sweetheart, have another swig of this, and I'll walk you down there, you're in a bit of a state.' He turned to his mates and left the bottle with Susan. After a while he said, 'Come on then,' he'd catch up with his friends later, and they set off, Susan was aware of some jeers and suggestions. He asked how she came to be in Harwich, she said she'd come with a friend in a car and she'd lost him. 'Never mind he said, plenty more fish in the sea, do you fancy a drink?'

Oh yes, every nerve ending screamed but she heard herself say, 'I need to get back to London.'

'Sure it won't be a problem.'

They came to a huge car park full of container lorries. He told her to wait while he went into a cafe. He was gone about ten minutes, he came out with a burger in a bun for her and pointed to a particular lorry. 'That's Stan's, he'll be good to you not like some of the scum. He's just finishing his dinner, when you see him going to his cab, go over. He's expecting you. I should sit here,' he pointed to a bench, 'then you can see.'

'Thanks for the burger, can I pay you?'

'Nah, had a little win on the gee gees.'

'You've been really kind.'

'Good luck darlin'.'

Stan was in his fifties, with thinning hair, a red face and a huge gut. Susan felt more in control, the food had helped. Stan would take her home, or at least to where she could get home. 'What's a nice young woman like you doing, hitching a ride?'

'I got a bit stuck, someone let me down.'

'You don't want to trust anyone these days. Lucky you found

me, I should have been off hours ago, they closed the yard, place has been crawling with police. Happening more and more regular these days, tip off I reckon, found a whole gang in a container from Holland, mixed they were, Afghans, Albanians, and God knows where else. Never get the real criminals though, just the poor sods who've paid through the nose to get here. Sometimes they get the middle men who come to meet them.'

Susan showed some interest, through her silent counting. Lamp posts, start again at every red light; hold breath through tunnels. They were on the motorway and she was feeling good sitting high with the force of the lorry like a tank to protect her, invincible she thought, I am invincible. Stan was a family man, lived in Barking, grown-up family, Sam, short for Samantha, lived close with the grand-kids. Job was alright, got two days off a week, money OK, one or two perks. Stan liked talking and Susan could be a good listener. The traffic got heavier so she guessed they were coming in to the city. 'Where you got to get to?' he asked her.

'I live in Brixton, or I could stay with my sister in Stoke Newington.' Could she? What had made her say that?

'This lot's headed for Stratford, that's not far from Stoke Newington; you go and see your sister and tell her your troubles.' She got out soon after and thanked him. It was five o'clock and she really did want to see Jennifer. She went into a café near the station and ordered a coffee and a muffin. She'd have to wait to nearer seven to be sure Jennifer would be home.

She walked from Dalston working out what to say, promising better behaviour, saying she was only trying to help, begging forgiveness this once, or perhaps she should say once more. At seven twenty there was still no answer, she was shivering despite it being a warm evening, she was drenched in sweat, she vomited behind the wooden erection that Bill had made for his bike, and slumped down with her head in her hands. Maybe fifteen minutes passed and she heard a key being put in the front door, she scrambled to her feet expecting Jennifer but saw it was Bill on the doorstep. He was taken aback. 'Susan! God you scared me, what are you doing?'

'Waiting for Jennifer.'

'She's not here. Christ you look a mess, you'd better come in.'
She followed him in. Bill went straight to the kitchen. 'Aren't you coming in? Shut the bloody door.'

'I'm sorry Bill.'

'Not that again. What have you been doing, you look terrible. Have you eaten?' Susan said nothing. 'Have you been drinking?'

'No.' Should she have admitted the cider? She looked at Bill. He didn't look angry.

'Look Jennifer's in Romania, I've come to check on some work I've been doing. Why don't you go and get cleaned up and borrow some of Jennifer's things then we'll have a talk. I'll go out and get some food. Take your time.'

Jennifer's bathroom was perfect, she could spend hours there. She made a neat pile of her smelly clothes; chose the shower against a bath and stood for a long time under the gushing water. She used Jennifer's soaps and gels, washed her hair in luxurious shampoo, scrubbed her nails, borrowed a toothbrush, wrapped herself in a mauve, sweet smelling towel and felt like the person she wished she were. She delayed in the bedroom where she had found a pair of jeans and a tee shirt, nervous to go down. She could hear Bill cooking with the radio on.

'You needn't tell me if you don't want to,' Bill said. Susan did tell him, at least as much as she remembered, it had been coming back in snatches. She had been with Cornet drinking for two maybe three days, a real binge, then at the end of the third day he said he had work to go to and that she could come if she liked. She'd slept in the back of a car with Cornet in the front and another Romanian man driving. Then she woke in a flat, somewhere near Harwich and Cornet was gone. 'Harwich?'

'I hitched a ride back in a container lorry, he dropped me at Stratford and I came straight here.'

'You lead a dangerous life Susan.' He put a bowl of salad on the table and an omelette in front of her. She ate slowly. All day she had met kindness, the man who gave her a fiver, the cider-man in the park, Stan in the lorry and now Bill. Suddenly she was standing in church in Macclesfield between Mum and Dad, I am unworthy Lord, she had always been unworthy, they made sure she knew that.

They had coffee in the garden, the evening was still warm and the light only just going. Bill had bought her ten cigarettes, she could have kissed him. They lit some candles on the wall of the little patio and talked about Jennifer; Bill said she'd been gone for ten days, which was five longer than she'd intended, and that he was worried. Gradually the light faded and the smell of a neighbour's jasmine sweetened the atmosphere. Silence fell between them, then Bill stood up, blew out the remaining flickering candle, took Susan's hand and led her upstairs to the spare room, where, on this day of kindnesses, they were kind to each other before falling asleep.

12

Boian was in low spirits, alone, in his apartment; the old woman, the fire, Jennifer, the photograph, all plunged him deeper into chaos. He 'phoned Muller and said he had to go away, to see a relative, then he took the battery out of his phone and sat for days in front of the television, with curtains drawn, eating the last of his mother's stash of tinned food, and drinking beer. Night and day merged, television gave him the only sense of time, and he took little notice.

He left the apartment on the fourth day late in the afternoon. He drove his pickup to a track he knew that probably ended at the hut where he'd last seen the old woman. It took him some-time to find the entrance, no one had used it since the wood yard closed. It would be a hard task for his vehicle, the ruts were deep, dried in the summer heat to hard as concrete. The truck lurched from furrow to furrow eventually finding an equilibrium. The fur-ther he got into the forest the more he questioned the wisdom of his decision. He thought he would be safer in his vehicle, though he didn't understand why he should feel danger from an old woman and a tethered dog.

He took his direction from the sun, and drove west. At a fork in the track, one way dived steeply through dense forest, the other circled the side of the slope. If he got down the slope he'd never get back up so he chose the higher route. He drove very slowly, the road on the left hand side fell away steeply, he had to hug the right hand side and pray the road would hold. There was no going back anyway, turning the truck would be impossible. At every jolt he imagined himself rolling over the edge, and if he survived, who would find him, this forest had not been worked for thirty years or more? It was the other side of the village where the diggers were clearing the way for the new businessmen. He banged on the brakes just in time; there was no road, a tree had come down and demolished it. A few metres ahead he could see it begin again. He was stuck.

After a couple of cigarettes he got out of his cab and set off scrambling, falling, sliding down the slope; now the forest was so dense he could no longer see the sun. If he kept going down he had to reach the other road. A salamander flitted across his feet, the first life he had seen in this abandoned place. He reached the lower track and walked for ten minutes peering ahead and left, and thought he had missed the hut. It felt as if he was above and way beyond the village. Then he saw it, through the trees, in a small clearing, the back of the hut. He scrambled down. It looked empty, everything shut. As he got closer he could see the end of the dog's chain leading round the corner, he followed it round, trying not to make a noise. A crowd of flies rose and descended again, jostling for position on the carcass, the smell made him wretch; the dog was recently dead and still chained. Covering his nose and his mouth he edged close to the wall and pushed open the door. The shack had a veranda on the front, there were several buckets with flowers as dead as the dog and some garden tools. He edged past lifting his shirt to cover his nose and mouth. The door was open, inside were a stove, a couple of cooking pots, an unmade bed against a wall, a table covered with newspaper, two chairs and a chest, which he gingerly opened. It contained an old blanket and some stuffed toys; a bear and a rabbit. There were no clothes, except for a black coat hanging behind the door, and he noticed the old man's walking stick. The wooden floor was bare. He touched the stove, it was stone cold.

He took a spade from the veranda and at the side of the hut he scraped the last year's decaying leaves from a spot and began digging a hole, the earth underneath was soft and the edges of his hole kept crumbling in; he worked hard, sweating in the heat, the sun was on the wrong side for shade. Tying his tee shirt round his face he laid the blanket from the chest next to the dog and tipped him on with the spade, dragged him carefully to the hole and covered him quickly with the soft earth. Then he sat for a while, the quietness was immense, no birds. He imagined himself living there, perhaps learning to hunt, there must be something living in this forest, or perhaps living on berries and fungi. Not having to see anyone, especially not having to see Emile. He smoked the last of his cigarettes and set off towards the village following the

76

route he had taken a week ago.

Back at his apartment he went round to the parking area and took the cover off his moped which had stood unused for two years. He pushed it to the petrol pump, it didn't take much to get it going. At the café by the bridge he ordered a plate of spaghetti. 'Your brother was in earlier, bad luck about the fire' said the owner. Good thought Boian, he's unlikely to come back.

After his meal he ordered coffee and asked the owner about the old man and woman, the flower sellers from the bridge. 'She used to come in here didn't she?'

'Yeah, that's right, I think the old man died. What's your interest in her?'

'I found her dog scavenging round the bins, I tied it up, thought I'd best try and find her.'

'Best put a bullet in its head; Pieter might know, he did some work for one of her sons once.' Pieter was the cook, 'I'll call him out in a minute.' Boian sat down with his coffee.

Pieter came out drying his hands, 'Yes I know Olga; fallen on hard times, she lives in a hut in the woods behind the old button factory. We used to think she was a witch when we were kids, she had a nice house then. She went away for a long time.'

'Where did she go?'

He grunted a laugh. 'Where did anyone go in those days?'

'Do you know where she is now?'

'If she's not in the hut then maybe with her son in Suceava.' Boian explained about the dog and asked if he knew the address.

'Best shoot the dog.' He wrote the address on a napkin. 'Watch that son of hers, he's a bad lot.'

He waited for a while to get his breath back after climbing five flights, the lift was boarded up and marked DANGEROUS. He could hear the television on inside the apartment, graffiti was scrawled across the walls, *gypsy scum fuck off*. He knocked on the door, after a couple of minutes he knocked again and thought he could hear movement inside. The door opened a fraction on a chain and a man's voice said 'What do you want?'

'Can I talk to Olga?'

'Who are you?'

'My name is Boian, Olga knows me and my brother, and she's got something to tell me.' The door closed and there were muffled voices on the inside. Boian waited a while and knocked again. This time the door opened and he was let in. The old woman was on a sofa watching television, the man who let him in, her son, Boian presumed, was big, about his own age, his head was shaved, his face unshaven, he wore pyjama trousers and a dirty grey tee shirt.

'Ma, someone to see you.'

'Who's that?'

'It's Boian, we met in the café by the old bridge, and again at the hut, you said you had something to tell me.' He lied.

'I don't know you,' she said.

'Yes you do and my brother Emile.' She glanced at her son.

'I don't know this man.'

'Yes you do, you spoke to me, I've been back to the hut to find you, you've got to tell me what you know.' His desperation was showing, 'I'm sorry about your husband.'

She stood up, her face was burned dark from too many summers, she had rheumy eyes and a mouth that tipped down towards folds of flesh that buried her neck. She was short, maybe not five feet. She spoke with sudden strength and fury, 'Get out of my house, I don't know you.'

'I went back to the hut to find you. I buried your dog.' When this registered she turned to her son and spat some incomprehensible abuse at him, he shrugged and went into another room. She turned back to Boian and they looked silently at each other.

This time she whispered, 'Your brother knows more than he's told you, now get out or I'll set him on you,' she jerked her head towards the other room, 'and he's nasty.'

Emile was in the car park of the Carol at eight-thirty a.m. as arranged. It was a glorious morning, the sky a startling blue. 'Today we have some fun,' he said.

'I hope so. How far to the architect's office?'

'Unfortunately we cannot see him today, he is out all day on a site visit to a big project in the south.'

Jennifer was put out, was he lying to her? He was driving on his brakes and accelerator, screeching through town, and for the first time Jennifer wondered about her own safety. She hadn't been replying to Bill's messages, and no one knew exactly where she was. They were on a dirt track going up into the hills, either side of the track were houses in various stages of being built, but no one was working on them.

Emile stopped the car. 'Come see.' By now Jennifer was worked up into near panic. Emile got out and came round and opened the passenger door for her. 'Welcome to my house.' There was very little more than the foundations built. 'We go through the front door, I lead the way; here the big kitchen, all western appliances, beyond the dining area; here the family room, the kids watching the television or on play station. Here the grown-ups room. Upstairs, we can't go today, five big bedrooms and two bathrooms, what do you think? Good for a business-man?' She would not remind him that Merta had left him. This was about him.

'Very good,' she said, 'where are the builders?'

'Ach always excuses, they run out of materials, lazy sods; always money up front, money money money!' Jennifer thought about the factory and said nothing. 'Come, we walk now.' From the back of the house they ascended through a group of fir trees to a small clearing where two horses were tethered in an open shelter. 'Now I show you something.' He shouted across the hill and a teenage boy appeared with tack for the horses. 'You ridden before?'

'A long time ago.'

'The horses know what to do, you just sit there.'

They set off together, through a pine forest. Emile was full of smiles and boyishness, and Jennifer was ashamed of doubting him. She had doubted him before, at the airport; she beat her cynic into submission. The horses were sure footed and climbed steadily. Emile in front turned his horse to watch her as she left the tree line. 'You like?' The magnificence of the landscape left her speechless. 'Beautiful this country yes?' She could see spread out beneath her two mountain ranges. He led on, along a ridge above the trees, dotted about the fields beneath them were small farms with single cows and a few hens in the gardens. The fields were full of flowers, and in some fields family groups were work-ing with scythes cutting hay, loading it onto carts which were tethered to oxen. Jennifer gazed. It was the garden of Eden in a picture book bible. 'People have gone back to the land, it's in their blood.'

Back at the house the boy responded to a whistle and led the horses away. The plan was to have some lunch and visit the burned out factory. Jennifer wanted to see for herself. On the way down the hill Emile's phone rang. With the phone pressed to his ear he continued his terrifying speed down the mountain track. She could understand nothing, then she recognised the name Boian. Emile swung the car off the track and stopped, jolting to a halt as he continued to talk. Then all was silent. 'What has hap-pened?'

'Boian's truck has been found, in the forest on the other side of the valley, no sign of him.' Jennifer had not seen Emile like this. He was white, visibly shaken.

'Maybe he drove to do a job and got stuck.' Now she was the one making excuses.

'The police want to see me. I'll drop you at the hotel.'

'Emile, don't forget I am family, I will come with you.'

They drove silently, crossing the river and following its path out of town towards the village where these boys had lived and she had been born in the dark days of oppression. They passed the track into the forest, there was police tape all around it, and two officers standing by. He pulled off the road. 'Is there some-thing you haven't told me Emile?' Jennifer was frightened. She did not know this country and its customs but surely police tape to prevent entrance would not be appropriate just because a truck had been discovered. As they sat in silence a tractor pulled out of the entrance towing Boian's truck. It was a sharp turn right and one of the police officers walked over to ask Emile to move his car. Emile started the engine and drove on towards the village.

'Emile if we are family then you must tell me what is happen-ing here; if I am not your blood, then take me back to the hotel and you will never hear from me again. I thought it did not mat-ter, that we could be good business partners irrespective of fam-ily connection. Now I see that things are complicated and there is much that I don't understand. If we are blood then I want to understand, if not . . .' He took her hand.

'I think you are my sister.' Jennifer felt her eyes prick with tears. 'I was told that there is a hut near where Boian's vehicle was found, outside the hut the police have found some graves, they are in the process of exhuming them.'

13

Susan woke between laundered sheets full of fresh smells; there were no clothes littering the floor of her room; in her patch of sky there were little white clouds dancing. Ignoring the mess in the kitchen, she brought tea back to her flowery bed, sitting up against her pillows, holding tight to every little detail of her night and morning with Bill. He had bought her breakfast in a café; he hadn't been embarrassed; he had kissed her when he left. She recalled the sensation, and knew she should not play it too many times, its intensity was already fading. He had asked if she needed money, and more, much more than that he had suggested she could make some money buying and selling, car boot sales and the internet. She could start a little business and he would help her, and he didn't mention her problems at all.

Bill woke in a cloud of guilt. What had he done? She had looked so frail and vulnerable out on the patio. Two good reasons not to have taken her to bed. Perhaps it was him who was vulnerable. She had lain in her deckchair, dark hair falling in curls around her temptingly pale face. But he knew it was her frailty that had overpowered him and that, in a way, Jennifer's strength unmanned him, and that Susan was not to blame. What a mess. Yesterday had gone by and she had not called him, perhaps she was ashamed too, after all it was almost incestuous for her he argued illogically, trying to shift blame. Best if they both forgot it. He would have to see her some time but felt sure they would come to the agreement that it had never happened. Meanwhile what to do about Jennifer?

Susan topped up her 'phone and scoured the free newspapers for car boot sales. There was one at a local school on Saturday. She'd start there, with a few things on a table. She felt sure Bill would phone today, she'd ask him for some books. Maybe some of her old clothes, there was a leather coat Jen had given her. Jen would have piles of stuff, she pictured the bathroom with all its bottles and her wardrobes over full with fashionable clothes. Perhaps if she went there again with Bill . . . no that was a bad thought. When Jennifer got back and saw how industrious she was she would be bound to help. Maybe she would have her own shop one day, 'Vintage Clothes' in Camden Passage, her dream rolled on, but her 'phone was silent.

Bill busied himself with his emails, dealt with his sales, found ordered books and began parcelling and addressing, in time for the midday post. His 'phone rang. 'Hello Sally', he recognised Jennifer's work number. Sally said that Jen had contacted her to say there was no problem but she was going to have to stay in Romania a little longer; she'd asked Sally to tell Bill. 'How long?'

'She didn't say.'

'Do you have a location for her?'

'No but we text and email for business decisions.'

'Yes of course.'

'You've got her number?'

'Yes, yes.' What a stupid question of course he'd got her number, they'd been together for ten years.

'Bye now.' He jabbed at his parcel and the Stanley knife cut his finger, damn, now there was blood everywhere he'd have to begin wrapping all over again. Why hadn't she texted him direct? She wanted him to know, so there was a meagre flicker of something to remind her he might just be a little concerned. Damn her!

Mid-afternoon and Susan had run out of things to do. She'd spent twenty minutes making her bed and her slippers were placed at right angles directly where her feet would land. She'd bought food and a bunch of flowers for the kitchen table and looked at her 'phone at least every five minutes, when suddenly, joy of joys the bell, the lightest of hope-filled sounds; a message signal. *Hi Susan, sorry about the other day, hope you got home safely, in a bit of bother and need £250, sorry to ask. Bumped into an old friend who might have some news of your sister. Love, Cornet.*

It was dawning on her that Bill was not going to 'phone, that she had in some way disappointed him. Her plans seemed suddenly ridiculous, impertinent even. She could hear her house mates chattering in the kitchen and although she was hungry she couldn't face them. She sat in front of her newly tidied dressing table and saw the ugly, drawn woman looking at her. Someone in the house always had gear for sale, she could get some downers and sleep. That bell again, but not working its magic. She left it without looking, she hadn't got money for him and she didn't care much about Jennifer who hadn't been in touch for weeks and had left the country without any message. They could all fuck themselves, when it was quiet in the kitchen she would try and do a little transaction, she found her purse. The message on her phone flashed. *It's a lovely evening, fancy a walk and a bite to eat?*

Fuck off she typed and did not see as she pressed send, Bill's name at the top. Dan was in his room and counted out her pills from a cardboard box and took her fiver. She declined his offer of more grand delights. She took a glass of water from the kitchen and swallowed the pills. On her bed with curtains drawn, the little snatch of consciousness remaining was peaceful, so wonderfully peaceful.

What had he done to warrant that?! He was furious and hurt. The woman must be more bonkers than he'd given her credit for. Well she could fuck off too, he was well out of it. After work he called a male friend recently divorced, they met in a pub and talked football, books, films, travel and finally bloody women; a subject that inspired them through several pints. He left the pub at ten o'clock, it was only just dark and still warm though the pavements were wet from a recent shower. He was drunk enough to be not absolutely steady on his feet but not so drunk as to be unaware of it; in one particular lurch he ended up in a privet hedge which dripped water all over him, but feeling vindicated by his recent conversation, he laughed and felt rebelliously male. He stepped off the pavement and did not see the blur of grey metal and light shimmering in black reflecting glass. He did not hear the screech and squelch of wet tyres on tarmac, or the siren's wail.

He came round in the ambulance, he was strapped onto a stretcher, and had a drip going into his arm. Someone was talking from a long way away.

'Hello, hello, Bill, you're OK, you're going to be OK. Are you comfortable? Hello, hello, Bill, are you awake?' He swam in and out, he'd been in a forest wrestling with a man who hit him and sent him spinning into a lake, but the trees were still there in the lake and someone in a boat was trying to push him under with an oar. There was noise, wailing all around, he was dragged from the water, tied with ropes, lots of people talking. 'Semi-conscious, in and out, theatre's free. Hold on old man you'll be OK.' Darkness.

Susan crept back into the world at two p.m clothed and sweating and needing to vomit. Eyes closed, felt her way to the bathroom, three steps to the lavatory. Vomit. Count ten for the water to run warm, plug in basin, count seven both hot and cold together. Wet flannel and wipe face, armpits, chest. Cold tap, one, two, three, four, five, squeeze and wipe; back in her room staring at the hag. Dan would be out she guessed, she would have to wait for more oblivion. She waited and a vision of after school club flashed across her mind and the anxiety of whether she would be remembered or not. Her 'phone was dead, no credit. She put on a jacket and looking nowhere and at nobody she went to the shop, topped up her 'phone and bought a bottle of wine to tide her over till Dan's return.

No new messages, she wondered about Cornet, he must be somewhere near to suggest a walk last night. Maybe she should see him, she pressed the button to retrieve his texts. She could lie and say the *fuck off* was meant for someone else. Be good to have some company. She stared at the 'phone. Nothing made sense, what was she reading? Something had got muddled in the system. 'Oh fucking Christ,' she said out loud. It dawned, Bill had invited her for a walk and she had told him to fuck off. She pressed Bill's number. *Hi can't get to the phone etc.* Bill's voice, her heart leapt, but not Bill. The shop phone, ringing, on and on, he should be there it was only four, maybe he'd had to go out. It would be all right, she could explain.

The doctor told him they'd had to pin his leg in three places, that he'd been very lucky, that the driver of the car was in shock. He'd be in the hospital some time, and then physio'. 'Do you play

85

sports?'

'I ride a bike.'

'Well not for a while,' the doctor said. A junior came to clerk him in; next of kin? Mum and Dad. Contact? I'll call them. Girlfriend? Not really. Work? For myself.

There were four others in the ward. His bed was nearest the huge window. He could see beyond the Eye and the Gerkin as far as Greenwich. He was in the Royal Free Hospital in Hampstead, he'd no need to ask. Yes, he'd been drinking in The Eagle on Rosslyn Hill, it came back to him in segments. He slept a great deal throughout the day.

Susan reached the shop at five. She could see the blind down and the closed sign as she approached. She asked in the café, no they hadn't seen him since yesterday, no he hadn't said he was going away. Cosima knew where he had a room, she'd found it for him, Thornhill Road, it wasn't far away. A smart middle-aged woman answered. No, he hadn't been home last night. He must be at Jennifer's. It was seven when she got to the empty house in Stoke Newington. She had a kebab in the café opposite at the table where they had had breakfast, and he had kissed her goodbye. Why do I fuck everything up? she said to herself, and let the tears fall onto her plate.

14

Well if Emile was mixed up in some shit, what was it to him? Emile was always mixed up in shit. If the shit was worse this time, that's his look out. Boian drank his second plum brandy and ordered a third in a corner bar outside the flats. He would go back home, if his moped could make it, and tomorrow he would borrow Old Müller's tractor and pull his truck out of the forest and go back to work for him. Emile could stick his sales manager bullshit, big ideas, it wouldn't be long before he had him shovelling shit, well he could shovel his own shit.

The young woman behind the bar filled his glass and smiled at him, Boian returned the smile. She must have been about eighteen, born to freedom, so called. Government tyranny replaced by gang tyranny, some fucking choice. He considered chatting her up, she looked willing enough, but he wasn't in the mood. His eyes flitted from time to time to the window and his moped which was parked on a side road. There were lads roaming the streets in twos and threes. He didn't think his ancient machine would have anything attractive for them but it would be a bloody nuisance to find a wheel gone.

'Where are you from?' The girl behind the bar asked.

'North of here, near Vatra Dornei.'

'What's it like there?' God she's chatting me up Boian thought!

'Very beautiful, you want to come home with me?' She leaned over the bar and practically put her tits in his face.

'Maybe?'

He sat back on his stool to get the full picture, and check the window. His bike was surrounded by four youths . . . 'Hey. . .' He yelled as he ran out the door, he turned the corner to see the moped being wheeled away down a side street, he ran after them shouting, they turned another corner and were out of sight, he followed and tripped, someone pulled him into a garage and the door shut. 'What the fuck . . .?'

Thump in the stomach, 'That's for asking too many questions,' smash to the side of his face, 'that's for interfering' kick in his balls 'that's for being nosey,' he crumpled over in pain, a few more kicks and he heard them running off.

He lay there groaning for a while then he heard the door open. He tried to hide behind an oil drum. The girl's voice, 'Hello, are you in here?' he crawled from his hiding place. 'Oh God, they've made a mess of you.' She helped him up.

'How did you know I was here?'

'I followed you, saw them trip you, I couldn't do anything, I'm sorry.'

He limped over to his machine, it looked OK, 'Oh no! They've slashed the fucking tyres.'

'What are you going to do?'

'Fuck knows.' He sat on a drum.

'My aunt takes in guests, not far from here, and her husband would know a garage for your bike.' She said. 'You can't go like that though.' Recent and past experience didn't encourage trust, but what options did he have? He let her take charge, she smuggled him in the back of the café and he washed himself carefully. He had to wait in the café until she'd finished her shift, then she took him by bus to her aunt's place. She said he was to say he'd been in a road accident, calling as she crossed the road to catch the bus back, 'Good luck, come and see me again.' He didn't even ask her name.

His bike was repaired the next morning; they were a straight couple, didn't ask questions, he paid them and set off for home. He chose the unmade roads which were potholed and excruciating on his testicles; he went very slowly and stopped a couple of times for a drink and food, and to find petrol.

Back in his flat everything was as he had left it; sad and empty. The water was hot though, some things remained from the old days, often radiators were on full belt throughout a thirty degree summer. He stood in the shower, then gingerly hugging his knees close in the confined space he sat down and let the water pour over him for about half an hour. He erased all the messages left by Emile and Muller without reading them, and went to bed and slept.

'Do you know of any reason why your brother should have taken his truck into the forest?' The policeman leered over Emile as though he had committed some vile crime.

'I've no idea, I haven't heard from him for a couple of weeks. But that's not unusual,' he added hastily.

'When did you last see him?'

'I said, two weeks ago.'

'That before or after the fire?'

'It was before but what's that got to do with anything? If my brother's missing shouldn't you be looking for him?'

'Don't worry, we are.' Emile didn't like the implied threat but there was little he could do or say. The policeman seemed to get bored after a while and Emile was allowed to leave.

After his long sleep, Boian ignorant of local events, went into town on his moped. He had a woman friend who worked in a printing office and would do him a favour.

She looked at him strangely, 'Thought you were missing.'

'What gave you that idea?'

'Some news about your truck in the forest.'

'Oh yeah, well it got stuck.' He wondered how it could have been found. 'I want a favour sweetheart.'

'You always do.' He produced the christening photograph that he had taken from his Dad's house and asked her to scan it and email it to him.

'What do I get?'

'I'll bring you a present back from England.'

'You going to England?' He didn't answer, but she did what he wanted.

'You watch it, there are people asking a lot of questions about you.' He wondered who was asking and how they had found his truck. He'd have to look into it later, now he had something to complete. He drove to the other end of town to the only internet café. Not many people in there; he created a new email address *clearasday,* then copied the photo across and sent it separately to Emile and to Jennifer, with no message, then went home to wait for developments.

Behind The Carol was a park with tarmac paths, clear paved edges, benches and shelters. All new, for the invisible tourists. The trees were a hundred years old, planted when The Carol and its park were the summer residence of some aristocrat, all now incorporated into the new town planners' idea of a thriving spa, yet to find visitors. The trees shaded the local children on scooters and bikes, and couples, young and old, arm in arm. Jennifer walked beyond the park to where the ground rose quite steeply, she followed signs directing the way to the ski-runs. She found a simple chair lift, incongruous in the sunshine. Inside the waiting shelter the chairs were stacked close. She chose one of the least steep runs and continued her climb. She should go home, back to London, she knew that, yet she could not leave this story, her story, behind. She also couldn't help feeling in an irrational way that she might be in danger. Not out here alone, but with Emile and his not quite straight answers. He said he thought she was his sister, what lay behind that? She had wanted this family so much, this romance, she knew she had not gone carefully or asked, demanded even, proof. Bill would have been more careful, would have made her more careful, and deep down she probably believed Bill and his research, that her mother was some Liverpudlian prostitute.

She had wandered off the ski slope, and tired she sat for a while in soft grass and flowers. Of some she knew the names, violets and primroses, and others, tiny with white and red flowers, were they called scarlet pimpernel or had she made that up? And wood anemones, a favourite. Perhaps she could come back in winter with Bill for the skiing, somewhere fresh and new and away from the madness of the Alps where they usually went. Oh Bill, what had she done? She needed to know for certain if she was born here, if these men were truly her brothers. She had been operating in a fantasy, wanting to believe and being prepared to believe, craving a history, a descent. And now things seemed deadly serious and she felt herself out of place. She liked Emile, but too often she wondered if he was telling the truth. She desperately wanted to see Boian, she felt he was trustworthy. *Well get a fucking DNA,* Bill's words returned to her. She had to do this, she would look into it. Surprisingly her telephone had a signal, she typed *Hi Bill,* but the next phrases all sounded wrong in her head, after much thought she continued, *things are a bit worrying out here. I am deeply regretting turning down your offer of help. If you could come for a few days I would be really grateful. Fly to Cluj, ask Sally to fix it. I know I don't deserve it,* which she changed to, *deserve you. Love Jenxxx* . She turned back, taking a different route down, feeling clearer, lighter, she even ran in places.

She passed the two sour faced receptionists, who were often too busy, at God knows what to give any help, with a cheery 'Good Morning'. No smile cracked their facades. Up in her large room she turned on the television and drew back the net curtains to look over the park. In the background the music of a language she didn't understand, but hoped to, one day, babbled from the TV. Emile was calling for her in an hour, this time they were going to see the architect. Her ears caught the name of the town she was in, Vatra Dornei; the picture was of a hut in a forest, clearly a crime scene, men and women in plastic jump suits, her heart turned over, this must be where Boian's truck was found, an interviewer was talking with a policeman, then the picture changed to a truck being towed along a forest path. There could be no doubt. Was this National news, or a local station, did it matter? The bitches downstairs would give her no information that was for sure, she had to wait for Emile. The hour dragged slowly by. Her high spirits replaced by a fearful dread, she looked out at the mountain in the distance. During a holiday in France one year, she and Bill had dared one another to go off piste, later they learned four skiers had been killed, doing just that, by an avalanche close to where they had been. She had rather hoped for a return message from Bill. If she hadn't sent him a text, she would be packing for home right now. Yet she had to know who she was, she had a right to know, for certain, yet she hated certainties; there is a God, there isn't a God, two sides of the same rigid mind. Nothing could be certain ever, life was a series of best guesses, except DNA, but even that was statistical.

She saw Emile drive his Renault into the car park just below her. Relief and apprehension were a queer mix. They met in the foyer, he asked if she was ready and at her nod they walked outside. They sat down on a shaded bench, not many people around, maybe because it was lunch time, or too hot at this time of day.

Whatever news Jennifer was about to hear she was glad to be outside. A woman passed with a small terrier, it lifted its leg on the bench, the woman called it sternly and apologised, Emile made light of it.

'Let's walk a little in the park,' Emile said, 'we are not expected at the office for half an hour.' His mood was sombre, no sign of the little boy of yesterday.

'There has been some news.'

'I saw Boian's truck on the television but I couldn't understand what they were saying.'

'They have found the remains of eight infants, babies, buried around the hut, probably been there for thirty years or more. There may be others, they are still searching, there was also a dog, buried more recently. There is a clear trail from where Boian's truck was discovered, of someone sliding down the forest bank to the clearing. There is a full blown search on for Boian.'

They sat in silence. 'I don't want to go to see the architect, I want to arrange a DNA test to see if we are related, and then I must return to London. I cannot be away from my business there any longer.'

Emile held her hand, such a comforting gesture, 'Yes, of course,' he said.

15

The pain kicked in on his second day in hospital, the doctor had said it would be like this, and Bill, feeling vulnerable had given permission for his parents to be told. He had grown up in Oxford, his parents meeting at university there had never moved away. His dad was a partner in a GP practice and his mum was a psychologist, His one brother, with whom he had nothing in common, was something in IT. A nurse came to say they had phoned and would be visiting him later. He thought he probably should tell Jennifer.

He saw his family enter the ward, they were peering rudely at other patients, trying to locate him; he was embarrassed, like on sports days, or when they came to see the school play. They were always so bloody confident and spent more time patronising other parents, and worse still teachers, and never seemed very interested in his achievements, and a 2:1 degree in English didn't impress them over much as an achievement. Nevertheless his dad hugged him, saw him wince and asked some medical questions, while mum held his hand, and his brother, the elder by three years, said, 'Bad luck old chap.' They could see he was in pain and didn't stay long. His mother asked about Jennifer, Bill said she was abroad on business but would be home soon. She didn't ask any more questions but found his clothes in a plastic bag and took them saying she would be back tomorrow with new pyjamas and a dressing gown.

He couldn't sleep for the pain, he had to stay in one position, and the drugs were not having much effect. He summoned a nurse to ask if he could have more, but apparently he was on the top dose; the staff nurse, Rodney, came to see him, and asked him if he'd like a little walk, Bill thought he was taking the piss. Ten minutes later Rodney returned, released a break on the wheels of his bed, and pushed Bill out of the ward. 'What's this about?' Bill asked, Rodney told him it was a little constitutional and it might help the pain. They went along a wide corridor where friends of the Royal Free had an art exhibition, into the lift, along more corridors, past a drinks machine.

'You fancy something?'

'No thanks.'

'This helping?' It was, he couldn't move but somehow the movement of the bed relieved his pain.

'You done this before?' Bill asked.

'Fancy going out?' Bill was getting the idea and didn't question. He was pushed through two rubber casualty doors and into the car park, dodging vehicles, and managing ramps, round to the back of the hospital. It must have been about two a.m. on a warm June night, the air smelt of exhaust fumes from the night busses, and taxis on Rosslyn Hill. Two days and a few hours ago he'd been there. 'Do you want a ciggie?' Bill said no, he didn't smoke but promised not to tell. Rodney sat for a while on a low wall, smoked, and asked Bill about himself and Bill told him about Jennifer, the love of his life, about how they met, their travels in India and the Far East; Jen's business; his shop; their new house and how good life had been before some crook from Romania had insinuated himself into it. He told him about her sister Susan, but not about his mistake.

'No wonder you had a night on the booze mate, things sound pretty bloody complicated. Have you told her you're here?' Before they headed back to the ward Rodney had promised to put some 'umph' in Bill's 'phone, rescued unbroken from his pocket, after the accident. The conditions were that he kept it on silent and only used it to text; strictly against the rules, but as he couldn't walk to a 'phone, Rodney thought allowances should be made.

Bill was almost asleep by the time he was back in the ward. When he woke, his 'phone was beside his bed with its battery full. The ward was waking up, breakfast smells and trolleys rattling. He pulled the 'phone under the covers and pressed the messages button. One from Susan saying, *Hi Bill, where are you? Last message meant for Cornet not you. BIG MISTAKE, please get in touch. Sxxx* The other message, from Jennifer, had been there for thirty-six hours.

His mother came early bringing a Harrods night shirt, shaving equipment, towels, tissues, facecloths, electric toothbrush, all smiles and practicality, and left behind an aroma of Coco Chanel, and a promise to return with Dad at the weekend. Susan arrived in the afternoon bringing a bunch of flowers that would have filled several wards, an enormous box of chocolates, with satin bows and ribbons and a plastic bag dripping with grapes; she sat down by the bed and started crying. 'It's all my fault.' Bill's heart fluttered. He reached for her hand and told her to stop. She did look lovely when she was sober. She gently touched the bandages on his face. 'Does it hurt?'

'Bit sore, I've eight stitches just above my eye, but they said it will only be a hairline scar, legs a bit of a problem area.' He told her the extent of his injuries and she began crying again, so he told her about the doctor delivering the bad news and good news – good news being, he still had two legs; he made her laugh. She fed him chocolates and grapes and went away to bother the nurses for vases for her flowers. When she came back she asked him if he wanted her to do anything about the shop, she said he could trust her. 'I've heard from Jen,' he said. At this moment Susan was glad Jen was off the board; Community chest - Go to Romania. Chance - Stay in Romania for another month for big business deal.

'Oh right. How is she?'

'I think she might be in some trouble, she's asked me to go out.'

'I thought you two were . . .'

'Yes we are but if she needs help . . .'

'Of course, but you can't go.'

'That's pretty fucking obvious.'

'Sorry.' They were silent for a bit. 'What sort of trouble?'

'She didn't say, but she's not the sort to ask is she?'

Susan wanted it to be about Bill and her, but how could it be, he still loved Jennifer. He was far more worried about her than concerned about himself. He imagined her involved with gangs, making silly decisions. Susan reminded him that she had never made a silly business decision, she was good at that sort of thing, she didn't say hard nosed, that would have been cruel. 'But why does she want me to go out there?'

'Have you told her about the accident?'

'Not yet.'

'Should I go out?'

'Would you?' He trusted her! Susan was overjoyed, she would go further than Romania for him, if he asked. They spent till the end of visiting time plotting and planning how to get Jen home in the context of their imagined scenarios and discussing practical arrangements. Sally would arrange tickets. When it was time to leave, he gave her money, and didn't tell her not to spend it on drink.

16

When the police swarmed the port Corneliu had attached himself to a group of Polish drivers. He left the depot under a tarpaulin in the passenger well and they dropped him in London at dawn. He was sorry to abandon Susan, he'd liked her, but right now he needed to disappear. He knew a relatively 'safe' house in East London. It had cost him some money but as far as he knew the police had lost his trail. He was on his own, dumped by those that worked him. He had seen others cast aside in the same situation. The police knew he was small fry, but they'd bang him up nevertheless. Maybe not for long but then they would probably deport him regardless of visa. It would be different if he'd got something to offer them but he'd nothing. Orders came by text, always different numbers. At this moment he thought it might be best to go home. England hadn't been so great. Perhaps he could go back on deliveries again, he'd pushed to get to do the U.K. side, now he thought one group a month across country would be easier, there was no pot of gold here.

Three of them were sleeping in the small back room on the first floor. Well, he wasn't sleeping which was why he heard the cars draw up at five thirty a.m. at the end of the street, and was out of the window and down the drain pipe into the neighbours' garden before the others woke, and before the dozen policemen started battering the door. He could run when he had to. There were probably bloody terrorists in the house. That was the trouble with 'safe houses'.

The sun was coming up, there was heavy dew on the grass and he was terribly cold. He was in a pavilion, next to some old geezer who'd pissed himself, nevertheless Corneliu would have appreciated his sleeping bag. This was his second night out, he'd got to make a plan. He jogged round the perimeter of the park to keep warm, the gates were not open yet, the place was familiar, it was where he had shared a bottle with Susan, in what seemed ages ago but would have been only two weeks. What a bloody ass he'd been to ask her for money. On his third circuit he could smell coffee, the gates were opening and so was the park café. He took himself to the conveniences, made himself look as un-derelict as possible and went for a coffee and bacon roll.

He must be near the bookshop where he'd met Susan, maybe she'd be back at work, if the bloke she worked for had forgiven her. He found his way down onto the Caledonian Road, at the prison end, and began walking towards Kings Cross. He found the shop, it had its shutters down and a notice on the door which read 'closed due to illness'. He asked in the café, Cosma told him the owner had been knocked over by a car and was in hospital. Round the back of the shop, he waited until the road was clear and quickly scaled the wall. The lock on the back entrance was pathetic. The duvet was still where they had stuffed it under the cupboard. On the sofa, under the duvet, where he thought he could still smell Susan, he slept.

He woke a few times, remembered where he was and forced himself back into his dream, it was dusk when he finally got up and took stock, his visa had run out, he had no money, no job and nowhere to live. He'd get no more 'people' work for at least a month, that's how it went after an incident. He reckoned he might be safe where he was for a couple of days. He found a cash box and forced the lid, he'd be able to pay it back, he'd get some kitchen work, no questions asked. He had to put money on his 'phone and get some food, he waited until dark.

This was not the worst situation he'd ever been in, at eighteen he had been put in prison for thieving, he was proud to have survived that, many didn't. In a way it made him, gave him a career, introduced him to foreign travel, gave him good contacts. He had met Emile in prison, he'd been caught joyriding in a party official's car, like the bloody idiot he was in those days. But Emile had a way with him, got on well with the big boys, they set him up, nice little business with plenty of space. Suited them both. When Corneliu was free and started as a courier he regularly delivered to Emile's factory.

Corneliu turned on Bill's computer and fiddled around, it didn't take long before he came up with 'biljen' and he was in. He celebrated with the one beer he had bought. At least he could play some games to pass the time, time until what? He banished the thought, something always cropped up. After midnight he got under the duvet. A flashing light disturbed him, the answer phone machine, he pressed a button to try and stop it. *You have one message; message received Wednesday 6th June at 4pm; Bill, where are you? So sorry about the text it was meant for Cornet, how stupid I am, please get back to me, of course we can meet up.* Click. Susan's voice. So Susan had replied to his text after all, maybe not pleasantly, but who knows? At least she had replied. He picked up his 'phone, *Dear Susan, sorry about everything, can we meet, love Cornet.* Everybody's sorry about something; he went back to the duvet a little more hopefully.

The road was empty and Jennifer's speed was more aggressive than exhilarating. It was going to be a week before she and Emile could get an appointment at a private clinic for a DNA test, despite all sorts of strings being pulled and bribes paid. She wanted them to fly to Hungary and get it done in a day but Emile kept saying he could fix it. Boian was in police custody, and no one was telling them anything. Even Mr. Fixer with his bribes couldn't get anywhere on that one, and now to cap it all her bloody sister was about to arrive at Cluj airport. 'Had an accident,' Bill had said, probably twisted his ankle, bloody hypochondriac, she blamed his mother – but why in the name of all that's holy did he have to tell her sister to come out? Well, if she had a drink she was going on the next 'plane back. Jennifer fumed at the wheel of the hired Mercedes.

The airport was well signposted so she had no difficulty in finding it; the car park had plenty of space and the building was smart, modern, friendly almost. She sat in a café where she could see passengers emerge from arrivals. The coffee was good, she was tempted to smoke, everyone did here, but she'd given up years ago and it would send out the wrong signal to Susan. She read the boards, the arrival from London, Luton was on time. Passengers began coming through, the first ones, those with hand baggage only, looking focused and businesslike, those that followed divided easily into those arriving home and those arriving abroad. She saw Susan, black linen trousers with a turquoise shirt, flat black sandals, looking very smart. She was scanning the hall looking for Jennifer, and Jennifer felt she had taken her first breath since leaving Heathrow last week, she might be her bloody sister, but it was a bit of home, and she did love her. She walked over to her and the two hugged as though they would never let go.

Susan told her about Bill and the extent of his injuries and Jennifer felt guilty about her previous thoughts. She wondered how Susan had got to know about it, when she didn't. Susan said Bill had asked her to come out and made it all possible; with tickets and new clothes, Jennifer assumed. How things change. Jennifer then started on her story, the more she told the more absurd it sounded. Susan accepted it all with sympathy. She only asked how long she intended to stay in Romania. It was past ten but there was still some light as they drove through the long painted villages where the mountains behind seemed like the same painted cloth. They could not remember when they had last been in a foreign country together. Susan said Ibiza when she was sixteen, but Jennifer said she'd never been there.

It was late when they arrived at 'The Carol,' after such a long drive Jennifer wanted a drink. 'You have a drink Jen, I'm happy with coffee.' The bar was empty but lit and a waitress brought them what they wanted.

'Thanks for coming Susan, it means a lot, I feel much better.'
'I am still your sister.'

17

December 6th 1975. The back yard was covered in a thick layer of snow. Paul had been away all day working at the wood yard and had called off somewhere on the way home. Dana thought he might be seeing another woman, but she was past caring. She appreciated time without him in the house. Her life was hard to bear, as hard to bear as the baby she was carrying. In another month it would be here, another mouth.

Emile was playing a counting game in her button box, she gave Boian a crust to chew to prevent him from spoiling the game and cut herself a slice from the loaf and spread some fat on it. The wind blew fresh snow against the window, it blew the rags she'd put to keep out the cold, from off the sill, she pushed them back wedging them in the cracks more securely. There was not much food but at least there was no shortage of wood and the little kitchen was snug. She could keep the baby on the breast until spring came and food got easier to obtain. She sat down in the big chair; Boian tried to climb on her knee, but with her belly there was no room, she sang to him to keep him good, Emile crawled over and leant against her legs. She would get them to bed in a little while. If Paul didn't get back soon Emile would have to go out to get more wood for the stove, it was a hungry feeder on a night like this.

She was comfortable, the boys were calm and after a while she drifted off to sleep. The cold woke her, the stove was out, she didn't know how long she had slept. Boian and Emile were under their covers fully clothed. She stood up quickly to see if there were any embers left in the fire. Warm liquid poured from between her legs, her first thought was that she was peeing herself then she realised it was the baby, too soon, too soon. She had planned to have this baby in hospital, she was going to stay with her sister in the town from a week before it was due, this was typical of her luck.

The pains had not begun, if she could get the stove going

maybe Paul would be back. Perhaps she could hold on. With her clothes wringing wet she pulled on her coat and an old one of Paul's and holding the log box in one hand and feeling the wall of the house in the other she made the journey to the woodshed. The snow was high against the door, she shovelled it away, and took what wood she could carry. Back inside she was shaking with cold, and fear. There were embers, she piled in the wood, and left some for later, it would be warm soon. The waters were still running, she needed the midwife, how long could she wait?

Hail Mary full of grace, please let Paul come back, Holy Mary mother of God, don't let the pains come yet, Blessed art thou among women, keep me safe. I'm sorry for my bad thoughts about Paul, Pray for us sinners, now, OOOH her belly crushed in on her, help me Blessed Virgin. The spasm passed, she looked over at the boys, they were still asleep. She mustn't cry out. She pulled the mattress to the floor, the old alarm clock by the bed said ten p.m. Paul must be stuck in the snow.

Gingerly, before the next contraction she put a pan on the stove to boil putting a knife in to sterilize. Calmer now, she gave herself up to fate; what use was prayer when she didn't believe? She held onto the table for the next spasm and noted that it was fifteen minutes from the first, she had a while to go before things got too bad, she must prepare. She was convinced now that Paul was stuck, and that even if Emile was old enough he would not be able to get through the snow to fetch help. She checked the boys, and straightened their covers. She had things to do. A rubber sheet for the bed, towels to lie on, as she reached to pull the curtain between her and the boys another spasm caught her, she nearly cried out. She must try to keep silent. A bundle of cloths wound tight would do to bite on. She prepared in this way and then lay down to wait it out.

By one p.m. the contractions were every few minutes, she squeaked and Emile called out to her. 'Mummy's got tummy ache,' she said, 'put more wood in the stove and go back to bed,' she held her breath and heard him do as he was told.

Another interminable hour passed. Soon now she would have to push, she propped herself up and laid clean towels under her. Now with every spasm she bore down, biting at cloth and sweating, with the next convulsion her bowels gave way, nothing she could do, the next one was upon her, and the next, biting, silently screaming, don't let me die, Jesus Christ, don't let me die. And then whoosh, slimy, slippery, mucus, blood and shit and it was out and the pain gone. Unbelievably gone. She lay back unburdened, it was over. Leaning forward she touched the mess between her legs, and it was warm, with her knife she cut the cord, pulled gently and delivered the placenta. Dipping cloths in a basin of water she had placed earlier by the bed, she gently wiped the mucus and shit from the baby's face, it was alive but it didn't cry out, she wrapped it tight and drew its tiny face to her breast where it nuzzled. Emile had woken, he put his head round the curtain. 'The baby's come,' she said.

'Is it a boy or a girl?'

'I didn't check,' she said, 'go back to bed now, we'll look in the morning.'

The horses dragged the trunks through the snow as it got dark. The ways were twisted and the paths too narrow for a tractor. There were generators at the yard and the men worked the big saws, four to a trunk, slicing and building the planks into great piles. They broke off after each tree had been dealt with and drank tea and warmed themselves by one of the braziers, no shortage of fuel here, and the overseer was a generous man. At five o'clock, they were free to go. The weather was getting worse as the men clambered into the wagon, yet the tractor made small work of the deepening snow on the track home. In the village Paul got out with two friends and visited a bar. It was warm inside the tiny room, they sat on benches, snow from their boots making puddles on the floor and steam rising off their jackets. They drank plum brandy to get the warmth inside and were soon singing. A farm gang came in and there was no room to move, those near the door were constantly being elbowed out into the freezing air, a welcome change to the stinking interior of the bar where Bella was making such good profit.

Around eight Paul left, thinking to call at Hilda's house, he had bought some chocolates from a workmate, black market stuff and thought he would give them to her, there was not much doing with his wife in her condition and a man needs his comfort. Dennis, Hilda's husband, had been Paul's work mate, and it was at harvest the previous year that his arm had been taken off by the PTO on the tractor; the boss had found him the following morning.

She was pleased to see him and the house smelt of cooking; a chicken broth. He knew she had other callers and that that was probably the source of the chicken, but he didn't mind sharing it, or her favours. This woman was generous in all respects, in her delicious bed he sank his hands in her flesh, his face in her breasts, he groaned in ecstasy as she expertly touched and squeezed. Oh the comfort of it. It must have been about ten when he thought to go home. 'Stay,' she said, 'no one can be expected to get home in this.' He considered the two miles he would have to walk. It was a filthy night. 'Your wife will be fast asleep with your little ones, she won't welcome the disturbance.' It was true, that two miles, if he made it, could take him an hour or more on a night like this. She wouldn't want to be woken at midnight. 'Bella will be out at first light with his tractor, clearing the roads, go then.' That would be best, he could be home before they got up and get the stove going for breakfast, someone would cover for him, a favour repaid.

The tractor dropped him off at the end of his road. He felt happy, no reason to be guilty, he couldn't have been expected to get back on such a night. In sight of his house he heard his son's voice; Emile was at the gate, 'Daddy, the baby's come, Mummy doesn't answer, come quickly.' Paul pushed past. Emile was frozen, he had pulled his school coat over his pyjamas and put on his boots with no socks, he'd been at the gate for fifteen minutes.

Boian was whimpering in a stinking bed. Behind the screen his wife was unconscious and burning hot, a baby still nuzzling at her chest 'Christ Almighty! Emile!' He screamed, 'Get more clothes on and fetch help, we need Olga and the doctor.'

It took all morning. The doctor said Dana would probably not survive. Half the placenta was still inside and she had a severe infection. He examined the baby and miraculously found all well, 'Thank goodness,' he said 'it's a shame about her little arm, but

I've seen worse disfigurements.' He advised that she be found a wet nurse, and said he would register a healthy birth. He gave Dana an injection and said to keep her dry and cool and get her to the hospital as soon as possible.

A covered tractor took Dana the next day to meet an ambulance on the main road. Her mother took the boys to her house. It was four months before they were home again with their parents, and the baby never came back. The boys, being boys, got on with their lives.

18

His face was badly bruised, a cut above his eye smarted, thank God his teeth were secure. He'd seen them make a worse mess on others. The hot water in the shower felt good on his bruised legs and arms. Familiar feelings of guilt and embarrassment overcame him – his father used to beat him until he grew bigger than him – he had not a big enough palette to separate guilt from innocence, childish confusion from adult cruelty. Perhaps it was the same for everyone? It had been five a.m. when they released him and he had not been offered legal help.

He was embarrassed by his seeking for answers; had he not learned anything from a childhood where to tell, or ask, more than the time of day was to ask for punishment? Emile was coming over, Emile was at the heart of this, his brother, yet he did not trust him. He heard him knock at the door, 'Boian – brother.' Boian recoiled from his embrace. 'Oh God, they hurt you man.'

Emile followed him into the kitchen firing questions, 'What happened? What were you doing in the woods? Are you accused of anything? Where did you go? What did they do to you? Oh man, your face!'

Boian made coffee silently and when he'd placed two cups on the table and sat down he said, 'I was trying to find out what you will not tell me.'

'What man?'

'If Jennifer is our sister or not?'

'Well you've stirred up quite a lot with that one.'

'Well is she?' Boian yelled.

'Hey don't yell at me. I'm not sure, I think so.' Emile stirred several spoonfuls of sugar into his coffee. 'Someone contacted me, said my sister was in England and for a certain amount of money they'd put me in touch; I did nothing, but then you said the old man was going on about what was lost must be found and all that bollocks, so I paid and got her details, thought it couldn't hurt to send her a note. That's all.'

'That's all, and you mean the factory being torched, me being beaten senseless, twice, the old woman, dead dogs and babies had fuck all to do with it?'

'That's all I know man. The rest is your stuff. Anyway Jennifer is here now, and her sister, adopted sister, and we are having a DNA so I guess we'll discover if we have a sister or not, or at least if Jennifer is her.'

Emile was edgy, his body jerked, his eyes darted around the small, familiar kitchen but never touched his brother or rested anywhere. 'You need a doctor?' he asked Boian.

'Don't be ridiculous.' Boian was silent and Emile stayed, fiddled with his phone, drank coffee, didn't do, or say anything. Boian fetched a recipe book from a shelf, greasy pages covered in long ago childhood dinners with magazine pages stuffed in at random. He carefully opened the book and turned page after page.

'You going to cook us supper?' Emile joked. Boian found the photograph between the leaves and stared at it for some little while before placing it on the table before Emile. 'I've seen it, you sent it to me.'

'So who is in the picture?'

'Mum, Dad, you, me . . .'

'And?'

'Janufa I suppose.'

'With two arms!' Boian yelled.

'It's hard to remember, I was five man, Mum was away for a long time, we were with Gran, don't you remember?' Boian said nothing. 'When we came home there was no baby, it was still with the woman who looked after it.'

'Olga?'

'I don't know, maybe.'

'So who is the baby in the picture?'

'I don't know, man I really don't know. I knew a bloke, we met when I was away . . .'

'Prison?'

'Corneliu, Olga's son, he was a good guy; we had lots of talks, there was time we were on the same gang. I knew him after for a while, then a year or two back he went to England. Then he called.'

'Out of the blue?'

'Yes, said he'd found our sister, I did nothing, then you were hassling so I contacted her, and now it looks like the whole fucking lot's come tumbling down.' Boian had not seen Emile like this, Emile was always optimistic, the big plans, the schemer. 'I should go now, the DNA's booked for this morning so I guess we'll know what all this has been about. You want to come?'

Susan picked up Cornet's message before breakfast and couldn't resist replying that she was in Romania. She texted Bill as well to say that all was sort of OK and she thought they'd be a few days. Then she joined Jennifer in the mausoleum of a dining room where the same waitress from the night before brought them cooked meats and poached eggs.

Being with Susan had changed things. Jennifer was struggling not to admit it had all been a terrible mistake. These people no longer felt like her people. More than ever she wished herself back into her life at the office and evenings with Bill. She dreaded the test that might connect her forever to this cruel place. 'You look a bit down,' Susan said.

'Well it's a bit momentous isn't it? I just feel like running home, asking Bill to forgive me and bringing him back to Stoke Newington.'

'No!'

'What do you mean?'

'You should have the test, after all you want to know if they are your family don't you?'

In the back Boian sat huddled, his beatings were obvious. Susan said he should get arnica for the bruises, she said the police were bastards in England too and she had friends who had been beaten in police custody. And all for burying a dog, which was a really kind thing to do. Jennifer was in the front passenger seat, and Emile was driving, they were silent. The clinic was in Suceava, it took them forty-five minutes and eventually Susan's perkiness succumbed to the heavy mood in the Renault. They drove past the block of flats where Boian had found Olga, and the café on the other side. They pulled in and Emile asked the way from a passer-by. They were directed up a side road to a new, two storey building, the sign on the door said *Medicentre* in English and there was a list of treatments. Emile pressed the bell opposite *Analize de Laborator*, a voice responded and the door opened. They followed Emile up to the first floor.

The waiting room was bright, a picture window with vertical blinds dispersing the sunlight, overlooked the street. They were the only people there. A receptionist in a white coat sat behind a desk. Emile and Jennifer were given forms on a clipboard to fill in. The four of them sat silently; a strange group; Boian a bit of a shambles, unshaven with his bruised face; Susan, nervous with over bright lips; Jennifer, smart, controlled with her hair pulled tightly back; Emile, forced casual, a parody. They waited whilst the forms were filled and Jennifer's credit card registered, then the two actors were called separately into a cubicle for a swab to be taken whilst the witnesses waited, and within ten minutes all was done. They would be sent the results by email within three days.

19

It was March with the hard winter was behind them. Along the path in the little back garden daffodils were just beginning to open. Dana had planted them the previous autumn. She arrived in a borrowed car from the convalescent home. It was nearly four months since she had left the house that bitter December day. Infection had followed infection, pneumonia had gripped her and the doctors feared TB, but she had come through it all. A fighter they said. She had hardly seen her boys in all those months, once or twice when she seemed to be turning a corner her mother would bring one of them, then the fever would come again and she was isolated until a new antibiotic got a hold. She had never seen her baby, a girl they told her, and very bonny.

Paul used to visit her once a week at the start, but was not always able to see her, so his visits had got more sporadic and he had settled into a comfortable bachelordom, sending money each week to his mother-in-law, for the boys, and Olga for the baby, and having his regular visits to Hilda.

He had cleaned and tidied the house for her, he'd done his best. He lit the stove, 'It'll soon warm up,' he said, 'there's a rabbit stew for dinner.'

'Did you cook it?'

'No but I shot it.'

She was lost in a room that was once her domain. Her life that ended with a birth in this room, seemed to belong to someone else. She sat at the table that she had used to scrub daily, she recognised its grooves, the hole where Paul had dropped his hammer when putting hooks on the beams. She was divorced from it all, especially Paul. 'When are the boys coming back?'

'I'll fetch them later, after Olga has brought the baby.'

'Is she christened?'

'No we waited, it's arranged for next week, we called her Janufa.'

Dana was uninterested. He came and put his arm around her, she stiffened, he left her. She looked and felt like a visitor. 'You can take your coat off,' he said 'you are home.' If it wasn't for the thought of her boys Dana would have taken a kitchen knife to him right now, or herself. 'Hilda sent the stew, shall I put it on the stove?'

'If you want.' The scullery was getting warm, the stove burned well, she took her coat off and hung it behind the door and in a remembered pattern reached for her apron. She'd feel better when the boys were back and Paul went out to work.

'I've got the day off today to help with you and the children.'

'I can manage.'

A car stopped at the end of the road, Olga's voice, 'I won't be long,' and a door slammed. 'Well, all safe and sound, here she is, your little miracle, she's been no trouble, my lads are really going to miss her.' She held the baby out towards Dana who did not move. 'She's a little cherub, she's had her bottle, and she's clean. Shall I put her in the crib then, I see you've got it ready?' Dana hadn't noticed the cot made up with blankets in the living room.

'Ay,' said Paul, 'put her down.' Paul counted some notes from his wallet and handed them over. 'Tell Dimitru I'll see him later.' And Olga, not knowing what to do was relieved to get away.

The baby, unused to her surroundings, began to whimper, Dana still did not move. The whimper gained in strength and became a full wail. 'Hadn't you best see to it?' Paul said. She went to the cot and loosened the garments wrapped around the baby. She gasped and turned in fury on Paul. 'This is not my baby.'

'Don't be stupid woman of course it's your baby.' In proof, it seemed, the baby screamed louder and Dana flew at Paul, beating him. 'What have you done with it, where's my baby, I did not give birth to that.' She threw a look of hatred at the cot.

'For God's sake, you didn't even know if you'd had a boy or a girl. How could you possibly know whether this is your baby, but of course it is, whose else could it be?'

'Maybe I didn't know if it was a boy or a girl but my baby had arms!'

'It's your child, and mine. You can ask the doctor, he said defects like this are quite common, he said there were any number of causes, maybe you were ill while you carried her, or ate something poisonous, or took some drug. She's still ours and we must see to her.'

'You see to it, it's not mine.' The baby's crying had subsided while her parents argued. Dana had a vision of the shed, getting on for a year ago now, and her blood evaporated till she felt cold and weak. The telephone rang, Paul answered.

'Yes she's home . . . yes she's here too . . . a bit of a shock . . . yes I'll be there within the hour. Your mother wanting to know when I'm going for the boys.'

'I will not rear that child, you can take it back where you got it from.' The argument raged and the baby in the cot joined in again this time with more determination until she was red in the face, her little uneven arms beating the sides of the cot. Dana grabbed her roughly and Paul, thinking she was going to throw her, took the baby from her and left the house. 'It's just too soon' he said 'too soon.'

Left alone Dana wept drawing sobs from the place where her womb used to be. How could she not blame Paul who had brought all this on her? *Her* arms now battered on the cot, on the walls, on the door; in a frenzy she grabbed the cot, painted by her grandfather. It had served her and her sister, her sister's children and her boys, it would not serve a changeling. It was solid and heavy but she found the strength to pull and push it out the door and along to the garden shed where she would not see it. She shoved the blankets in a sack and left them there too.

She was calmer now. She put wood on the stove and looked at the stew, Hilda's stew he'd said, she hoped it might choke him, but the children would need their dinner.

The boys stood shyly in the doorway. How they'd altered in four months, Emile's trousers and jacket were too small, he looked like a clown. Boian, her baby, was a proper little boy now. Emile went straight to his toy box, looking for something, or checking that everything was there. Dana took Boian in her arms. 'What a big boy you are now, have you been good at Nana's?'

'Grandpa let me ride on his motorbike.' Emile said.

'He said I could after my birthday,' countered Boian and he struggled out of Dana's arms and went over to check what Emile was doing. Paul found something to do in the yard and the boys chatted and quarrelled while Dana laid the table and prepared their dinner.

Later, when the boys were asleep, Paul said 'Olga can't look after Janufa any longer, she'll keep her over the weekend but then she will have to come home.'

'That baby is not mine, I will not have it.'

'Well what's to be done?' Dana was silent. 'Olga works at the orphanage, maybe they will take it in, just until you are ready.'

'You don't get it do you? It's not mine, maybe it belongs to you and your fancy woman but I'm not rearing it. It can go to the orphanage or anywhere you want to put it just as long as I don't have to see it again.'

20

The text from Susan in Romania was unexpected and disturbed Corneliu. He considered phoning Emile. And it was time he moved on. He switched on the computer, News from Romania, on google: *'Babies' bodies exhumed; the bodies of 12 babies . . .what?* Click; why does it take so fucking long? . . *the bodies of 12 babies, buried in a forest in Suceava County, have been found by police following leads. Forensic scientists say the oldest corpse was buried in 1972 and the latest in 1982. The babies all died of suffocation prior to burial, they were between a few weeks and four months in age. Witchcraft and human sacrifice have been cited as possible reasons for the deaths but latest enquiries point to a trade in babies to the West. Several of the corpses appear to have had birth defects leading to speculation that these were not acceptable for sale. A 76 year old woman, Olga Grosu and her son Dennis Grosu are at present in custody helping with enquiries. A second man was released.*

Jesus fucking Christ! Yet maybe he had always known, home from school, hearing babies crying, two to a cot, up to six at a time. When Mum was out, led on by Dennis they would poke the babies to make them cry, or undress them to find if they were deformed. They were living in the forest then, Dad ran the wood yard, Mum worked in town in the orphanage, babies were always coming and going, some stayed a few weeks, others only days.

He was trapped, danger everywhere; in England, banged up on some charge and then deported home to perhaps worse, but what had he done? An adopted Romanian child with withered arm, right age, could be Emile's sister, might get him a few hundred whether she was or not. Just followed a hunch hadn't he?

It was time to leave, and leave no trace, he removed the note that he had written and left in the petty cash promising repayment and took the rest of the money. He stowed the bedding where he had found it, washed his mug and plate and returned them to the cupboard, gathered all debris into plastic bags, stuffed his few belongings into his rucksack, wiped surfaces and left quietly by the back door. Several streets away, before descending into the tube he put his rubbish bags and his telephone into a refuse bin.

He was lucky in Harwich, a driver with a load for Hungary owed him a favour and a stowaway in the back of the cab under bedding and a crate of coke would be safe enough to get him across the channel, then he'd be all right.

Emile took them for lunch in town after the visit to the clinic, he knew a place in the main square, recently opened, western bistro style, stainless steel and mirrors, surprising to find such a place here, here where the best one could expect was escallops straight from the freezer; there were actual fresh vegetables and a good wine list. Emile ordered two bottles of white Rioja, drinking and driving was not an issue and nor was smoking in a restaurant, Susan smoked with Emile, who introduced them to the owner. Boian looked awkward out of place, badly dressed and beaten.

The waitress offered the wine for tasting and then poured out four glasses, Susan did not refuse. Emile suggested that he and Jennifer visit the architect's office the following day. He said the plans had been approved and once the finance was in place the building could start immediately. Clearly he felt, as Jennifer once had, that the results of the DNA were immaterial.

'There has been some news from London,' Jennifer began, 'my partner Bill is in hospital following a car accident, and I really need to be with him.'

'That's terrible, very sad, what happened? Many accidents here too, the driving is so bad.'

Susan cut in with the story of his accident, and the extent of his injuries. She talked of him to own a bit of him. Jennifer continued, 'It's not fair to leave him any longer, I was thinking of a flight tomorrow.'

Susan was drinking, Emile was agitated, Boian was silent.

'We meet first thing in the morning, I collect the plans later and bring them with me. Yes?'

'Don't you want to know if you're related first? What was this morning all about?' Susan blurted.

'This is a bona fide business proposition, and besides I have no doubt you are our sister. I feel it here,' he touched his heart, 'and Boian too, yes?'

115

'Maybe our sister was one of the babies in the forest.' It was the first time Boian had spoken since they'd sat down.

'What? What are you talking about?'

'I'm talking about the dead babies.'

'Yes man but what has that to do with us?' The women were silent, Susan filled their glasses from the second bottle. Jennifer was losing control, at the same time she wanted and didn't want more information. Susan was no help. The waitress brought their meal, Jennifer had chosen quail, it was presented beautifully on mashed potato with a sauce and surrounded by tiny florets of broccoli. Susan had pasta, 'Bon appetit!' The conversation returned to mundane matters, Emile ignored Boian, Susan tried to draw him into conversation, but he remained silent for the rest of the meal. A third bottle was consumed and Jennifer was soon business planning, discussing outlets and marketing. Yes, she would find a flight as soon as possible but sure, she would meet Emile first thing. Pudding was refused but not a little brandy on the house.

Emile drove carefully back to 'The Carol'. Jennifer annoyed that Susan had been drinking, and slightly drunk herself, ignored her and went to her room. She would find flights, and text dear Bill.

Susan let Jennifer take the lift, she waited for the metal gate to clang shut and the grinding mechanism to begin. She stepped out into the sunshine, she was at that stage where another drink was imperative, so much to block out. The pavement was uneven where a repair had been started and then abandoned; she was careful. She already knew where the licensed supermarket was, the habits of addiction were strong. On the way back she sat on the bridge and sipped brandy from a bottle concealed in a paper bag. The river bed beneath the ornate iron work spanned two hundred yards or more but at this time of year the water ran down narrow rivulets so that islands formed sprouting trees and shrubs; everywhere litter, plastic bags flying like flags off their tree poles. Her body eased and her mind numbed, she was only here and now. People passed, they looked at her, she was different, but she didn't care. Someone sat next to her on the bench, she stayed gazing over the dead river till he spoke to her in English. 'You like our town?' It was Boian.

'Hi,' she hid the bottle, 'such a nice afternoon, Jen went for a sleep, I wanted a walk, it's beautiful . . .' she trailed off.

'London must be beautiful? Big Ben?'

'Oh yes, bits of it, but bits of it are shite.'

'Shite?'

'I mean rubbish, sorry, bad swear word.'

'Shite here too,' he said. She was surprised how smiley he was without his brother. 'Shall I show you the town? Some bits not so shite.' They set off, towards the railway station and the shops, and the main street, away from the Carol. They crossed the railway line that ran parallel to the river, more like a tram-way being open as it was to the pavement. A short paved pedestrian road brought them to the main street. Brutal concrete architecture leant against domed, eighteenth century, decorated buildings; some, like the Transylvanian bank, gorgeously restored but most crumbling. Boian pointed out a café that was good for coffee and cakes and new shops selling expensive clothes and shoes. Susan looked down at her own feet in the smart black sandals she had bought with Bill's cheque, dusty now in the welts and her nail varnish beginning to chip. They sat on a bench beside the derelict synagogue; a nineteenth century, Moorish revival building with crumbling plaster but still with gold paint in relief on the Moroccan windows and rotting doors, bolted across with an iron bar. She asked where the Jews worshipped now and felt very stupid when Boian said there were no Jews here. He said the government were proposing a fund to turn it into a museum but he felt they should mend the roads first.

He smoked and offered the packet to Susan, sheepishly she brought her bottle into view, they drank together, told stories, talked and made mistakes in translation. When he was at school, near where they were sitting, he said the boys would come here to drink, if they ever managed to get their hands on any. She asked if they could go and look at his old school but he said it had been knocked down, together with the orphanage that was next door to it.

'Did my sister go to the orphanage before she was sold?'

'I don't know what happened to my sister.'

117

'Do you think Jennifer is your sister?'

'I don't know.'

'She's done all right, everythings goes right for her,' Susan was slurring her words, 'she's got money, an a housh, an a boyfriend who loves her. Now she's got brovvers, praps.'

Boian said 'Come I walk you back to the hotel, we can cross the river further up and walk back on the other side.' They put the bottle in the bin and Boian took her arm to steady her.

21

Seventy-two hours after leaving Harwich, Corneliu was in his own country for the first time in five years. He had passed through The Netherlands, Germany, The Czech Republic and into Hungary with no questions asked. His second lift took him to the border where he picked up a ride for the last leg from a Romanian, called Sorina with a transit van full of machine parts bound for Bistritsa. She was middle-aged and did most of the talking. He told her he'd been in Budapest for the marriage of his brother to a Hungarian woman. His mind wandered as she went through the births, marriages and deaths of her extended family. Then she was talking about the babies, and the woman they'd got for it, and how all the bad things from the old days were coming to light.

'Have they charged anyone?'

'They are still holding the old flower seller, seventy-five years old, must have thought she'd got away with it after all this time. They questioned her son then let him go, but he must have known something; cruel old bitch, hope she dies in prison. Yes, that son would have known something, he'll denounce her, they always do. Must be gypsies I reckon.' Corneliu held his tongue. 'My mother had five kids, you had to in those days or risk some-thing worse, and nothing to feed them on, luckily two died, natu-rally mind, no funny business; people were desperate. You come from near there did you say?'

'Yeah, not far.'

'You just got the one brother.'

'Yeah, Mum and Dad are both dead.'

She offered him a meal with her family after she'd made her delivery but he said he'd go to the railway station, then he could get back today ready for work tomorrow.

'What do you do?'

'I'm a chef,' he said, 'at a restaurant in town.' He immediately regretted it.

'Glad you're not coming for a meal then, what's it called where you work? I'll look you up if I'm delivering that way.'

'I work at the Carol Hotel.' He thought there was no likelihood of her actually coming. 'Thank you for the ride.'

'My pleasure; I enjoyed the company.'

He had forgotten 'the fear' he felt it as soon as he was on his own. He marked everyone, like a good field player, yet looked at no one. If Dennis wasn't home he'd have to break in. Dennis heard the knocking. 'Bloody journalists! I'm not opening the door, fuck off.'

Corneliu was loathe to broadcast himself, he said his name quietly into the door crack, 'Open the fucking door will you, it's me.' The door opened a fraction.

'What are you doing here?'

'Let me in for Christ's sake. Not much changed then.' Corneliu said, looking round.

'Not in the flats. Why did you come back?'

'Heard the news.'

'That's a reason to stay away.' Corneliu wandered round the small sitting room, he looked and touched a pottery model horse on the dresser on his way to the kitchen, he took a beer from the fridge and came back.

'You got anything stronger?'

'Brandy in the cupboard.' He made no move to get it for him and a relationship formed over years of abuse and minor violence was immediately re-established.

'How's Ma?'

'They didn't let me see her.'

'They charged her?'

'Not yet.'

'The old man?'

'Dead.'

'Dead?'

'That's what I said. Three weeks ago.'

'Cheers.'

'You going to see Ma?'

'Sure and end up with my teeth knocked into my balls in a police cell.'

'Why did you come back then?'

'I missed the home cooking.'

'Things not so good in the UK?'

'Brilliant, gotta penthouse flat and been shagging Madonna.'

'Like here then.'

'Some guys do very well, benefits, mobile phones, card fraud, I was in the wrong business, wrong bosses.'

'They know where you are?'

'Nope.'

'You'll be in trouble.'

'Someone ratted, I had to make a run at the port, whole fucking lot shipped back. Albanians, Afghans. Beautiful women man, should have made a packet.'

'So, not your call.'

'It would have been my call if they'd got me, fat lot of help I'd get.'

'You get paid?'

'Strictly cash on delivery, it's rubbish man, gotta find something else. What you been doing?'

'Got this nice little printing business.'

'Printing what?'

'Money.'

'Give over.'

'Doorman at the *Blue Mountain* bit of drugs on the side.'

They sat across the table from one another, and despite a childhood spent intimately connected in their fear and loathing of their father, and being separated for six years, they had nothing more to say. At ten o'clock Dennis went to work, Corneliu wandered round the apartment after he had gone; he opened the door to the balcony to try and get a breath of wind and noticed an old bike without wheels that had once been his, and a defunct washing machine and other debris. He was hungry but didn't feel inclined to go out. He found bread and toasted it. There was jam but no butter. He watched some television, there was nothing about the babies on the news, stories come and go. He woke from a dead sleep on the sofa to the sound of Dennis's key in the door. It must have been about three a.m.

'Look what the wind blew in.'

Dennis turned on the dim overhead bulb and Corneliu peered

at the other man. They shook hands. 'Corneliu man, it's been a long time. Bumped into Dennis at the club, he said you were home.'

Dennis fetched three glasses from the kitchen cupboard and produced a bottle of plum brandy from his pocket. They sat round the table. The flat had trapped all the heat of the day and it wasn't going to let go. Dennis' trousers were belted underneath his huge belly, he took off his jacket, his shirt was drenched. Corneliu wished now that he had showered while Dennis had been at work. He had a growth of beard, dirty clothes and he stank of days travelling. Emile managed to look cool in a blue silk shirt and pressed trousers, only his shoes had a little dust on them.

The conversation was of old contacts, friends lost. Commiserations on dead fathers and sympathy for Olga's situation. 'She'll cope, they can't prove anything after so much time, they'll be happy to drop it, too much shit happened, best move on.' Dennis said. 'Doubt she had much to do with it anyway, not so sure about the old man, he'd have cut his dick off and sold it if the price was right.'

'What got the police onto it?' Corneliu asked. Dennis was silent.

'You should know.' Emile said.

'What do you mean?'

'You must have ferreted around to find Janufa, talked to people.'

'I told you I talked to no-one. It was chance. I met her sister.'

'Yeah yeah, you might only have farted but it still stinks of shit.'

Corneliu stood up, his breath was short, a combination of heat and anger – fucking Emile in his fucking silk shirt – Dennis pulled him down and refilled the glasses. 'Haven't you got a fucking fan?' Corneliu growled.

Dennis talked about two girls at the club who had pissed off the owner, getting customers to wait for them outside rather than taking them upstairs; they'd done a runner, the men speculated on what would happen when they turned up. Nasty bastard, Big Den. It was a source of hilarity at the club that Big Den was five foot seven, whereas Dennis was six foot and eighteen stone.

'How's things at the factory?'

'You're out of it man, the factory went two weeks ago, torched. You were well out of it, fucking Janufa's fucking sister in London; I tell you, you should have stayed there.'

Corneliu sucked air in between his front teeth, a habit Emile remembered from prison days.

Corneliu had found Janufa by chance, but he'd called his mother to check a few things, now he was beginning to panic. Whom had she spoken to? Was he blown? The old paranoia welling up. Don't talk to anyone. What if Olga had talked to someone, mentioned him, someone checked, the Harwich delivery got compromised, a tip off, maybe aimed at getting him caught? He was sweating badly. No it was too far-fetched, and the cargo more valuable than his paltry life.

'Anyway, the sister's here now so she must be keen. Not for much longer though so you'd better get on with it. A wedding? English, nice and Legal?' Emile mocked.

'You gotta face like an arse and you talk shit.' Corneliu interrupted

'For Christ's sake you two, I thought this would be a happy reunion.'

'I'd better go, it's getting light, or did it never go dark? See you man, best keep out of the way a while, good luck, I mean it.' He left and Dennis shuffled off to his bedroom leaving Corneliu and the bottle at the table.

Jennifer was waiting in reception and was furious. When Boian and Susan reached the hotel, he kissed her lightly on the forehead and carried on along the river bank. Susan concentrating hard walked around to the main entrance. Jennifer by this time was in the car park. 'Where have you been? I've been worried sick. You can't just wander off on your own, this is a difficult country.' Susan stayed still and swayed slightly. 'You're pissed! I should have known I couldn't trust you, anything could have happened.'

'I wash with Boian, sight-seeing.'

'How did you . . .where was . . . never mind, we've missed a bloody flight tomorrow because of you; I needed your passport number to book it, and now it's too late and we'll have to stay here another day.'

'Sorry.'

'Oh for God's sake! I'll get you a coffee, you look ghastly.' Over coffee Jennifer said, 'Got a text from Bill, he wanted to know how you were, I said you were being a brick, should have known it wouldn't last.'

'Give over Jennifer, it won't happen again. How is Bill?'

'His legs are full of metal, says it's going to be fun when he has to go through passport control. Worried about riding his bike.'

'Did he want to know when we'd be back?'

'Of course, he's stuck where he is for at least another couple of weeks and his mother's driving him crazy.'

'Don't tell him about today, I promised . . .'

'Mmm.'

After a pot-full of black coffee they went to Jennifer's room to book the flight for the day after tomorrow. Jennifer was calmer now that she knew when she was going home. She replied to some business emails and Susan went to the bathroom and redid her nails with Jennifer's stuff. She needed to be doing something to abort the demons that said Jennifer's won again, she's had her adventure and now she'll leave Emile in the lurch, Boian in trouble, she'll take Bill back and you'll be all on your my own again. Always the same. Sitting on the edge of the bath she used the hair dryer on her bright-red nails and listened to Jennifer's nails tap tap on the keyboard. She had to beat this drink thing. She'd got to beat it even if she couldn't have Bill. Jennifer called from the bedroom. 'Shall we see what's on the menu tonight, or should we try somewhere else in town?' Susan pictured an aperitif in the bar, a shared bottle of red, couldn't do any harm, all Jennifer's friends did that.

She stood in the bathroom doorway and said, 'Do you know how all this business started?'

Jennifer looked up. 'From an email, Emile found me, you know that.'

'But what if the DNA is positive? What about the dead babies? There used to be an orphanage in town, it's been knocked down, you can't just leave all this as though it never happened.'

'If the DNA is positive I'll hear when I'm in England and my head will be clearer. The murdered baby thing is very sad but nothing to do with this; it's just coincidence.' Susan marvelled at her certainty. They went into town for dinner and Susan drank Pepsi Cola.

22

At six the following morning there was a knock on Susan's door. She sat up and said nothing. The knock came again. 'What do you want?' There was a reply in Romanian then silence. After a minute she heard something being pushed under the door and footsteps retreating. On a folded sheet of paper, in English, *Meet me on the bridge at 6.30. please. Corneliu.*

She found herself counting her heartbeats, she thought he was in London; did she want to see him? What did he want from her? She was meeting Jen for breakfast at eight-thirty, so she could go and be back in plenty of time. She would be safe out in the open and Cornet was her friend. She got dressed, the sour faced one was at the desk, should she leave a message for Jen? No, she'd be back before she was missed.

The sun was shining, it was cool with a light wind as she walked along the side of the river, she could see the bridge ahead, it looked deserted. It was six-thirty exactly when she began walking across it. Two women were walking towards her carrying buckets and mops, probably bound for The Carol or one of the other hotels on the south side. There was no sign of Cornet. She would walk slowly to the other side and if he did not turn up then she would go back. At the north bank she watched a train pull into the station and before it disgorged its passengers she was turning to retrace her way across river when her arms were suddenly pinned behind her and she was lifted, dragged across the railway lines in front of the train and forced into the back seat of a car which sped off immediately.

She was squashed between two men, her arms still held, she struggled and yelled, the man on her right, held her face harshly in his spare hand, turned it towards him and said 'You make another sound and I hit you very hard, maybe you lose those pretty teeth.' She smelt the booze on his breath.

She was quiet, the two men in the back stank of sweat and dirt. One was wearing cheap jeans made from flimsy denim, the other had jogging trousers, they were around thirty, she could only see the back of the driver. Where was Cornet? She was rigid with fear and an overwhelming sense of stupidity; if the note had been from Cornet that's how he would have signed it. And she had left no note for Jennifer.

'Where's Corneliu?' she said hoarsely.

'Who's that?' the jeans man said and laughed.

She should take note of where they were going, but they'd left the town and were on an empty road, just fields and more fields, mountains in the distance. The sun was to their left, but what the fuck did that mean? She was counting, breathing, every pothole felt like the car was splitting, counting helped, the stink was overwhelming.

'I'm going to be sick.'

'Fuck!' Then something in Romanian and the car bumped to a halt on a grass verge. They shoved her out and held her whilst she threw up. Jogging pants man passed her a bottle of water and she was manhandled back into the car. There was some conversation between the men, then one of her captors put a pair of sunglasses on her, except they weren't sunglasses, they were totally opaque. Her arms were still held, and the glasses too big to see above or below. The car was going slower, stopping and starting, she could hear other traffic. So they were in a town and she mustn't know where.

The car stopped and she was taken down some steps at the back of a building and into a cellar. Concrete floor and walls, no window, a grill high up, a bed along one wall, a table, with a bottle of water and a small fan. One of the men was with her, the jeans man, he was dark, almost black, small, but she knew to her cost that he was strong. He had her handbag and was looking inside at her things, she tried to grab it but he pushed her back, he took her 'phone then threw the bag on the bed, he left. 'Wait,' she screamed. She heard the door lock behind him, key and bolt.

She looked at her watch, it was ten to eight. Ten to eight and the room was unbearably hot. The wall opposite the bed was made of breeze blocks, perhaps an internal wall. She began to count them, ninety-seven and she came to a dangerous looking socket protruding, she connected the fan, it sort of worked.

Jennifer cursed her for not meeting for breakfast as arranged. She didn't rush her breakfast. She mused on the fact that however lacking a country's cuisine might be there was usually a satisfying breakfast; this was no exception, there were boiled eggs, soft and hard cheese, some sausage and salami, wonderful fruits of the forest jam and good coffee. Nine-fifteen and Susan still hadn't arrived. She called her mobile, no answer. She started fuming at the supposition that she'd hidden some drink away and was now comatose. Serve her right if she left her there and went off by herself for the tourist drive they'd planned.

She returned to her room and called her again. She banged on her door, she persuaded a maid to let her in. Where the fuck had she gone? The bed was crumpled and she noticed a piece of paper lying on the covers. It was the note. Fuck fuck fuck. Back in her own room, her heart beating loudly, trembling, she called Emile. 'Susan's gone.'

'What?'

'Susan's gone,' she explained the note, 'I must go to the police.'

'No wait, I must find out some things, don't do anything or go anywhere without telling me, I need a couple of hours.'

'What if she's been kidnapped? I can't wait.'

'Yes please Janufa, please wait.'

Back in her room Jennifer cried and cursed. Cursed her stupid gullible sister, cursed Bill for sending her out, cursed herself for the whole bloody debacle. Should she be waiting? What if this were giving her abductors time to get far away? Was she jumping to conclusions, maybe Susan was just off the rails again, this time with bloody Cornet or whatever he was called? Perhaps she'd gone off somewhere with him and then found her 'phone had run out; something simple and bloody annoying, just like her sister.

Jennifer calmed down, persuading herself all would be well and making sure she had her 'phone in her bag, she went out for a walk. She too, like Susan three hours earlier, walked along the south side of the river. The sun was hot now and getting hotter, the street full of people, a constant stream crossed the bridge, trains frequently rumbled past on the north side. Half way across the river she sat on a concrete bench and looked over the balustrade, where the water hardly flowed. The islands that formed were full of the rubbish of a modern urban society. She'd seen much worse in India. She was sitting on the bench where Olga and Dimitriu sold their flowers, before Dimitriu died and Olga moved to live with her older son Dennis. Jennifer knew nothing of this, nor of how her beginning had been intimately bound up with the sly pair. When in the early nineties, television footage of Romanian orphans hit the West, it is true she had wondered if that was something she had escaped, but it touched her no more nor less than the many fantasies she had created as a teenager. Susan had connected her being 'found' to the murdered babies crime of the mid-seventies. Jennifer found herself frightened; what she had dismissed out of hand now seemed to have a logic. 'God, Susan 'phone, please 'phone.' She said out loud. Her 'phone rang, she fumbled incompetently in her bag, why hadn't she kept it in her hand? She got it; Emile. 'Have you got news?'

'Yes, we have to be careful, and we need money.'

'Where is she?'

'I know where she is, we will need money.'

'Can't we go to the police?' Now in those seconds Jennifer re-lived the crushing doubt she had experienced at the airport. Should she believe this man? Brother or no brother? 'How much money?'

'One thousand euros, maybe we do it for less, but one thousand to be certain.'

'Then what?'

'I will come to your hotel in one hour, be in your car with the money, and passports. Take nothing else.'

The voice in her head; Bill's voice? Her mother's voice? This is a scam, this smells bad, you are being taken for a ride, fleeced, go to the police. She listened to the voice all the way to the bank. He said bring nothing else, how lucky she had Susan's passport to book the flight. She put the money in her laptop case, slung her bag over her shoulder and left the hotel. 'See you later,' she said as she passed the desk.

As she slammed the door shut Emile was beside her. 'We have to go to town first, I will direct you.'

'Where is Susan? Is she kidnapped? Is that what the money is for?'

'If she was kidnapped it would cost a lot more money. Her friend Corneliu is in big trouble, they are using her to find him, turn left here please.'

Jennifer did as she was told, after a while he said to stop outside some flats. He came out five minutes later with another man who got in the back. She did not start the car. 'Tell me what is happening or I go to the police.'

'Please Janufa, luckily my colleague does not know English. Let us get Susan, then I will explain.' The man in the back, Jennifer had hardly seen him, gave instructions in Romanian which Emile translated and Jennifer followed.

The air conditioning did a good job, the heat outside was threatening to melt the tarmac. In the open fields the shepherds had built shelters of sticks and rushes to give them some protection. Men and women, well covered with wide hats worked strips of land, it looked feudal, or like a Breugal painting. She had fallen in love with a picture book. Her situation now was something she might glance at in a newspaper: *Sisters disappear in Romania* and not give another thought.

In her cell Susan was lying on the bed, she had emptied and refilled her bag several times, the note was not there, so Jennifer would find it. She knew Cornet had not written the note, but maybe he could help Jennifer find her. Exhausted and wet through, despite the fan being next to her head, she sipped water not knowing how long it would have to last. She drifted into a sort of sleep. She was growing onions, a magnificent crop, she had them in a basket that was like a pram and was wheeling them to market. No one came to buy, other stalls had vegetables and they had plenty of customers. Bill and Jennifer emerged from a crowd, yes they would buy but they needed to see that the onions were good. She took a knife and sliced one in half, a tiny baby fell out, she took another and another, more babies, perfect, tiny and dead.

Drugged, the water, Emile pulled her from the bed and half carried half dragged her from the room. She grazed her shins on concrete steps as he pulled her up and away. Doubled over he shoved her on the back seat of the Mercedes 'Drive, fast !' The car was moving as he sat in the passenger seat.

'What about your colleague?'

'Just drive,' snapped Emile, and barked directions, Jennifer obeyed. Susan was crumpled on the back seat. They left the city behind and were once more on the open road driving south, towards Bucharest, Jennifer recognised the road. Gradually Emile relaxed.

'Susan are you all right?' Susan slurred a reply, 'Is she drunk?'

'Drugged more like,' said Emile.

'Please tell me what happened, and where we are going.' There was silence, and as Jennifer stole glances at Emile, she thought he looked desperate. In his own time he began to speak.

'I am sorry that I called you back to Romania, in England you are free. Susan was taken by people who wanted to find Corneliu, he came back and disappeared. She was to be the way to him. Now you must go home and forget about us all.'

'But the factory and our plans . . .?'

'It is not the time.'

After a couple of hours under Emile's direction they pulled off the road onto a lay-by with a stall. He fetched them coffee and some cakes. Susan was conscious but stunned. 'This is where I leave you,' Emile said, 'in forty-five minutes you will be at the airport, there will be more flights than from Cluj, you will get back to the West.'

'But our things?'

'You cannot go back.' He pulled two envelopes out of his pocket, handing one over he said, 'It did not cost 1000 euros,' and the other 'this is our DNA result. Good-bye Janufa.' He hugged her.

'But...'

'Good luck to you little sister.'

'Did you have to tell where Corneliu was?' He walked away, Jennifer followed and returned the envelope containing whatever was left of the money. 'We will meet again.'

'Maybe.'

She helped Susan into the passenger seat and when she turned

Emile was nowhere to be seen.

They left the car at Hertz and on the way into the terminal build-ing Jennifer took the second envelope and tore it into small pieces and dropped it in a bin. Doubt was where she had lived for so long; it was where she felt at home.

23

Mid June, overcast and humid; Susan woke late. She had said goodbye at Heathrow at around two a.m. after Jennifer had bought her a new 'phone and paid her taxi fare to Brixton; now she lay in bed facing the rest of her life. She had gone to Romania to support Jennifer and had caused her great trouble and expense; yet, she thought that her sister was not entirely without selfishness. The rest of the house sounded quiet, the house mates must be working or doing what they do in the day. She wanted nothing but to see Bill, yet that would solely cause pain.

Jennifer had set her alarm for eight a.m. and by nine she was in the office looking at the mountain of work that had accrued in her absence. She batted the enquires about her trip effectively yet colleagues gathered all had not gone well. She asked Sally to get her appointments with the backers of the Romanian project. Mid-morning she telephoned the Royal Free Hospital for visiting hours and discovered that Bill had been transferred to The Royal National Orthopaedic in Bolsover St. She phoned there and learned she could visit at two p.m.

Bill, who had spent the morning being pulled, manipulated, stretched on various machines of torture, encouraged, or rather, not let off the hook, by the perfect prototype for a Roald Dhal gym mistress, was hobbling back to the day room on two sticks when he saw Jennifer. She was sitting at the far end of the room, further than he would have liked to travel. 'Hello.' Bill eased himself into a firm chair and Jennifer kissed him.

'Poor you,' she said.

'Glad you are home safe?'

Jennifer had thought she would tell Bill everything. Despite her business success he had always been her security, she relied on him, and now she had pushed him too far, she had been foolish, she would admit so. But the situation was alienating, the room had six or more patients, mostly in wheelchairs, mostly with visitors. Bill had acknowledged others as he came towards her, and Jennifer remembered how easy it is to become institution-alised. Once when she was in hospital as a child for something minor, she had cried when she left. She remembered her father had visited her one afternoon and spent the whole hour staring through the window into the garden of an adjacent mental health unit. She now found interest in the other patients and asked Bill about them. There were sports injuries, quite a few cycling and some work related accidents, one soldier injured in Afganistan. Eventually Bill said, 'Well did you solve your problems? Sorry I couldn't come, I was a bit tied up! Was Susan any help?'

'It was good to have her around. I've pulled out of the manu-facturing deal, the infrastructure is just not up to it.' There would be occasion enough to tell him the whole story, now was not the time. 'How about you? How did you get here?'

'By ambulance I think.'

'Don't be an ass.' He told her about getting drunk, and the ac-cident, but not the events leading up to it and Jennifer, knowing him not to be a great drinker assumed it was related to his dis-tress at their break-up. The tea trolley arrived, Bill knew the or-derly who placed a portable table across his chair, and poured two weak, just warm cups of hospital tea; Jennifer balanced hers on her lap.

'Wimbledon next week, that'll help pass the afternoons after the mornings torture.' They chatted on like two old friends, nei-ther able to open their hearts to the other and tell honestly the momentous emotional turmoil that each had been dealing with.

Bill said he expected to be in the unit for two more weeks and then there would be physio' visits to his home arranged by the local authority. Jennifer asked if he would like to come back to Stoke Newington as surely he would be more comfortable there, they could put up a bed in the sitting room. Bill said he had made arrangements with Camden authority for his after-care and it would fuck things up to change to Hackney, and simultaneously a lump appeared in both throats.

A fuss at the entrance to the room took their attention; Susan was hurrying down towards them, looking desperate and tearful. 'Oh God, thank God I've found you. Sorry, I meant to be here hours ago, I went to the Royal Free and you weren't there, they took ages to find out where you'd been moved to and because I wasn't next of kin and all that crap, they made all kinds of excuses not to tell me, I was getting hysterical, then this nurse came by who knew you and he said it would be all right, but I couldn't find this bloody place, and I got the wrong bus and it took twice as long. How are you? I've brought you some chocolates.'

'Lovely, mmm Ferrero Rocher, my favourite.'

'Oh I know they are shit, it was all they had at the corner shop,' and they both laughed, and Jennifer joined in.

'So how did you like Romania?'

'Jeesus! Has Jennifer told you everything?' Out of the silence which fell Jennifer said she had told Bill the deal was off but she was leaving all the details to tell when Bill was home and things got back to normal. Susan was warned off and another beat shrivelled Jennifer's heart a little more.

Susan couldn't sit still or stop talking, but she kept to safe subjects; how the furniture was just the same as in The Priory; the tight bitches at the Royal Free; how long they'd had to hang around at Bucharest airport; the bastard taxi driver who wanted a tip when Jen had already paid him and who didn't believe she hadn't got any cash. Then she had a rush of remorse. 'I haven't asked about you? Oh God I'm sorry, can you walk? Is the pain better? What's this place like?' Bill smiled and assured her all was well, and Jennifer said she thought it was time they should leave, they'd been there a long while and they shouldn't tire him. She got up and kissed him and gave Susan a meaningful look.

Susan looked for her bag which she'd dropped behind a chair, as she stood Bill caught her arm, looked straight at her and said quietly, 'Stay a little longer'. Jennifer turned, saw the gesture, heard the words.

'I'll come tomorrow,' she heard herself saying as her short arm steadied herself on the back of a tall chair, before her high heels cracking like gunshots down the tiled floor, obliterated everything.

Epilogue

Boian woke early on the day of the funeral. He'd put on weight since he'd last worn his suit and although he managed to fasten the waistband the trouser legs concertinaed into his groin and looked ridiculous. The jacket would do if he didn't fasten it. He found some work trousers that were acceptable. The rain slashed at his corner window, a day for a funeral all right. It was still too early to leave so he sat, too big for his suit, too big for his kitchen, awkwardly on a stool at the counter whilst the television droned in the other room. He was used to being alone but this morning his loneliness was profound and memories that had long since been denied access to his consciousness flashed triumphantly by and plunged him deeper into his depression. The honking of car horns aroused him and he went to the window, through the sleeting rain he saw that a sort of procession was beginning with the car horns replacing the traditional brass band. Eight months since he had followed the horse drawn cart carrying his father along this same road but it seemed to Boian like another century. He must go.

The coffin, carried in the back of Müller's truck, had passed his apartment block when he joined the gathering that straggled after it. Neighbours held back in respect and he slipped in behind Merta and the boys. The village streets were deserted except for this noisy cortège; who would be out on such a day? The compacted earth of the summer was turning to mud as the water ran in streams around their feet. Following behind the ten or so mourners were two cars, unknown to Boian, imported cars usually only seen in the city; a Range Rover, perfect for the wet conditions and a Japanese 'off roadster', a Nissan maybe. They too joined in the band. As the truck, the makeshift hearse, reached the church men from the group stepped forward to lift out the coffin. There was silence while the men waited and Boian realised that he should step forward.

Through the window of the church Boian watched a sparrow sheltering in a willow tree, the wind swayed the branch violently but the tiny bird, a thin little thing clung on, the priest droned, the village women responded on cue and Merta snivelled in front of him. Surely the priest could cut down on the liturgy for such a sparse gathering? An hour passed, the bird had flown or been blown off, even Metra's snivels had dried up when at last the sound system piped the exit hymn, and one by one the mourners passed the body. The coffin was closed, had been closed throughout, a photograph surrounded by plastic flowers was propped up at head level for those that wished to kiss or touch. The body had been dead for several days when it was discovered, the Ukrainian police force had been involved, then the body returned to the Romanian county police, and held by them for post mortem before being finally released for burial. Cause of death was a bullet in the head at close range.

The rain was reduced to a light drizzle as they set off for the graveyard, Boian, not for the first time, but certainly for the last, bearing his brother on his shoulders. The ground was slippery and he feared an accident, the priest led the way slowly, as he had pronounced the liturgy, but now with more necessity. The women intoned, in a tremulous cackling, a funeral song, as they followed on behind. They reached the plot without mishap and laid Emile beside his mother and father, three graves, as close as strangers.

The dozen or so followers now talked to one another as they made their way towards the village. Since Ana's mother was dead and buried in her fur coat, Ana had turned her back room into a café. Boian hovered outside, old school friends, Müller, neighbours from his apartment building, all gave sympathy for his loss as they passed by. Only Olga, holding on to Dennis's arm, passed him without comment. The rain had virtually stopped and Boian stayed outside to smoke. The factory opposite was almost gone, the bulldozers had been in, and the forest had begun to be cleared, Olga's shack demolished and no sign left of the final resting place of the little unfortunates. The investigation had led nowhere, and as no one had claimed the infants, it ceased, like so many other crimes, to be buried in the record books. His apartment building was next on the list for development, somebody was making big money, but it wasn't Emile.

He went inside to speak to Merta. The party was getting quite lively, Merta presided. She had lost weight, and done something with her hair; she had been grey, now it was blond and tied up professionally; she was wearing a tailored dark suit and fashionable boots. She greeted him effusively with kisses that smeared his cheeks and called Roul and Alexandru over to kiss their Uncle. Alexandru had turned eleven and was dressed in the smart new uniform of the high school. 'Hello Merta, how are you keeping?'

'Not too bad. What about yourself?'

'Same as ever.'

She turned away, clearly didn't want to speak to him, especially about Emile whose name he had not heard mentioned from anyone, as though there were danger by association, despite his being in his grave. The last time he had seen his brother was at lunch in town, about six months ago, Janufa had been there and her sister Susan. Three days later the girls and Emile had disappeared. He had hoped and prayed they were all in England. A month after that he had received a postcard from Susan, from somewhere called Windermere, there was a picture of a lake. She was on holiday she said, she hoped he was well and that one day he might visit England, and that where she was – in the Lake District – reminded her of Romania. She didn't mention Janufa or Emile.

The party was slowly dispersing, a few would stay as long as there was a bottle open. Olga sat in a corner, shreds of hair escaping from her scarf, streaking her face and neck, which seemed all one flesh. Her mountainous son sat next to her silently drinking beer. Merta left with her boys, the stragglers wished her and her family well.

Boian finished his drink and thanked Ana for the hospitality, embarrassed, he apologised for not offering his apartment, and excused Merta, he said he'd heard that she was living with relatives while her new house was completed. Once outside he heard the Range Rover start up, a sound between a purr and a roar, he and Emile had used to guess cars and motorbikes by their engine sounds when they were boys.

Merta was in the front passenger seat, Roul and Alexandru in the back. Boian changed his mind about returning home and went back inside. Ana was at a table with several neighbours chatting

139

about this and that in the way of all villages. At another table, silent as the grave were Olga and Dennis. Boian joined them offering a drink which was declined. No one spoke for a while. Then Olga said 'I knew no good would come of it, don't say I didn't warn you.' Dennis shifted uncomfortably. The bent wood chair, inappropriate for his bulk and hardly supporting him, creaked under its load. Boian reached in his pocket for his wallet, he took out a folded card and smoothed it out on the table and pushed it under Olga's nose.

'Who is that?' Olga peered sightlessly then pulled a pair of spectacles from her bag. She laughed, wheezing and shifting phlegm that had settled in her passages.

'Well, Dana, for a start, you recognise your mother don't you? And your father. You, and Emile, God rest his soul, but he always was a wild one.'

'And who else?'

'What?'

'The baby?'

'Oh God knows, borrowed for the occasion, probably rented for twenty-five lei, the priest would have cost fifty and then there was the photographer, quite an expensive day.'

'Why?'

'Evidence of course; they were after her, you're as daft as she was. At least Emile had brains.'

When Boian left the café the rain had stopped and the sun come out. He squeezed the photo into a ball in his pocket and screwed up his eyes against the brightness. The water ran in the gutters in clear streams shot with light; passing under a bush, droplets of shining colour delicious on his face, made his thin jacket damp. He was comforted by the sunshine; he would continue to work for Müller who was childless and getting quite old now; with all the new building that was going on there was plenty of work; business was expanding. This was a new beginning for Boian, his heart was light, his way clear, he was unburdened. He threw the photo' into a bin; after all, it was not his sister. She lived in England.

Images

The Author

Convent educated, Bardy Thomas grew up in a midlands village
and has spent a lifetime in the theatre, including working in Romania. Since bowing out as Dean of R.A.D.A. she has turned the
spotlight on writing, flitting between London and Dorset with her
husband and two dogs.

OTOGRPHIE *prise vers le NORD* ★ *point marqué sur l'esquisse du plan* ★ DEALUL (*loc*